RUFUS M.

OTHER YEARLING BOOKS YOU WILL ENJOY:

YEARLING BOOKS/YOUNG YEARLINGS/YEARLING CLASSICS are designed especially to entertain and enlighten young people. Patricia Reilly Giff, consultant to this series, received the bachelor's degree from Marymount College. She holds the master's degree in history from St. John's University, and a Professional Diploma in Reading from Hofstra University. She was a teacher and reading consultant for many years, and is the author of numerous books for young readers.

For a complete listing of all Yearling titles, write to
Dell Readers Service, P.O. Box 1045,
South Holland, IL 60473.

RUFUS M.

by ELEANOR ESTES

ILLUSTRATED BY LOUIS SLOBODKIN

A Yearling Book

Published by
Dell Publishing
a division of
Bantam Doubleday Dell Publishing Group, Inc.
666 Fifth Avenue
New York, New York 10103

ISBN: 0-440-70027-2

Reprinted by arrangement with Harcourt Brace Jovanovich Publishers

Printed in the United States of America

July 1989

10 9 8 7 6 5 4 3 2 1

KRI

TO TEDDY

CONTENTS

RUFUS M.

1

RUFUS M.

RUFUS M. THAT'S THE WAY RUFUS WROTE HIS NAME ON his heavy arithmetic paper and on his blue-lined spelling paper. Rufus M. went on one side of the paper. His age,

3

seven, went on the other. Rufus had not learned to write his name in school, though that is one place for learning to write. He had not learned to write his name at home either, though that is another place for learning to write.

The place where he had learned to write his name was the library, long ago before he ever went to school at all. This is the way it happened.

One day when Rufus had been riding his scooter up and down the street, being the motorman, the conductor, the passengers, the steam, and the whistle of a locomotive, he came home and found Joey, Jane, and Sylvie, all reading in the front yard. Joey and Jane were sitting on the steps of the porch and Sylvie was sprawled in the hammock, a book in one hand, a chocolate-covered peppermint in the other.

Rufus stood with one bare foot on his scooter and one on the grass and watched them. Sylvie read the fastest. This was natural since she was the oldest. But Joey turned the pages almost as fast and Jane went lickety-cut on the good parts. They were all reading books and he couldn't even read yet. These books they were reading were library books. The library must be open today. It wasn't open every day, just a few days a week.

"I want to go to the library," said Rufus. "And get a book," he added.

"We all just came home from there," said Jane, while Joey and Sylvie merely went on reading as though Rufus had said nothing. "Besides," she added, "why do you want a book anyway? You can't even read yet."

This was true and it made Rufus mad. He liked to do everything that they did. He even liked to sew if they were sewing. He never thought whether sewing was for girls only or not. When he saw Jane sewing, he asked Mama to let him sew too. So Mama tied a thread to the head of a pin and Rufus poked that in and out of a piece

5

of goods. That's the way he sewed. It looked like what Jane was doing and Rufus was convinced that he was sewing too, though he could not see much sense in it.

Now here were the other Moffats, all with books from the library. And there were three more books stacked up on the porch that looked like big people's books without pictures. They were for Mama no doubt. This meant that he was the only one here who did not have a book.

"I want a book from the library," said Rufus. A flick of the page as Sylvie turned it over was all the answer he got. It seemed to Rufus as though even Catherine-the-cat gave him a scornful glance because he could not read yet and did not have a book.

Rufus turned his scooter around and went out of the yard. Just wait! Read? Why, soon he'd read as fast if not faster than they did. Reading looked easy. It was just flipping pages. Who couldn't do that?

Rufus thought that it was not hard to get a book out of the library. All you did was go in, look for a book that you liked, give it to the lady to punch, and come home with it. He knew where the library was for he had often gone there with Jane and some of the others. While Jane went off to the shelves to find a book, he and Joey played the game of Find the Duke in the Palmer Cox Brownie books. This was a game that the two boys had made up. They would turn the pages of one of the Brownie books, any of them, and try to be the first to spot the duke, the brownie in the tall hat. The library lady thought that this was a noisy game, and said she wished they would not play it there. Rufus hoped to bring a Brownie book home now.

"Toot-toot!" he sang to clear the way. Straight down Elm Street was the way to the library; the same way that led to Sunday School, and Rufus knew it well. He liked sidewalks that were white the best for he could go the fastest on these.

"Toot-toot!" Rufus hurried down the street. When he arrived at the library, he hid his scooter in the pine trees that grew under the windows beside the steps. Christmas trees, Rufus called them. The ground was covered with brown pine needles and they were soft to walk upon. Rufus always went into the library the same way. He climbed the stairs, encircled the light on the granite arm of the steps, and marched into the library.

Rufus stepped carefully on the strips of rubber matting

7

that led to the desk. This matting looked like dirty licorice. But it wasn't licorice. He knew because once when

Sylvie had brought him here when he was scarcely more than three he had tasted a torn corner of it. It was not good to eat.

The library lady was sitting at the desk playing with

some cards. Rufus stepped off the matting. The cool, shiny floor felt good to his bare feet. He went over to the shelves and luckily did find one of the big Palmer Cox Brownie books there. It would be fun to play the game of Find the Duke at home. Until now he had played it only in the library. Maybe Jane or Joe would play it with him right now. He laughed out loud at the thought.

"Sh-sh-sh, quiet," said the lady at the desk.

Rufus clapped his chubby fist over his mouth. Goodness! He had forgotten where he was. Do not laugh or talk out loud in the library. He knew these rules. Well, he didn't want to stay here any longer today anyway. He wanted to read at home with the others. He took the book to the lady to punch.

She didn't punch it though. She took it and she put it on the table behind her and then she started to play cards again.

"That's my book," said Rufus.

"Do you have a card?" the lady asked.

Rufus felt in his pockets. Sometimes he carried around an old playing card or two. Today he didn't have one.

"No," he said.

9

"You'll have to have a card to get a book."

"I'll go and get one," said Rufus.

The lady put down her cards. "I mean a library card," she explained kindly. "It looks to me as though you are too little to have a library card. Do you have one?"

"No," said Rufus. "I'd like to though."

"I'm afraid you're too little," said the lady. "You have to write your name to get one. Can you do that?"

Rufus nodded his head confidently. Writing. Lines up and down. He'd seen that done. And the letters that Mama had tied in bundles in the closet under the stairs were covered with writing. Of course he could write.

"Well, let's see your hands," said the lady.

Rufus obligingly showed this lady his hands, but she did not like the look of them. She cringed and clasped her head as though the sight hurt her.

"Oh," she gasped. "You'll just have to go home and wash them before we can even think about joining the library and borrowing books."

This was a complication upon which Rufus had not reckoned. However, all it meant was a slight delay. He'd wash his hands and then he'd get the book. He turned and went out of the library, found his scooter safe among the Christmas trees, and pushed it home. He surprised Mama

by asking to have his hands washed. When this was done, he mounted his scooter again and returned all the long way to the library. It was not just a little trip to the library. It was a long one. A long one and a hot one on a day like this. But he didn't notice that. All he was bent on was getting his book and taking it home and reading with the others on the front porch. They were all still there, brushing flies away and reading.

Again Rufus hid his scooter in the pine trees, encircled the light, and went in.

"Hello," he said.

"Well," said the lady. "How are they now?"

Rufus had forgotten he had had to wash his hands. He thought she was referring to the other Moffats. "Fine," he said.

"Let me see them," she said, and she held up her hands.

Oh! His hands! Well, they were all right, thought Rufus, for Mama had just washed them. He showed them to the lady. There was a silence while she studied them. Then she shook her head. She still did not like them.

"Ts, ts, ts!" she said. "They'll have to be cleaner than that."

Rufus looked at his hands. Supposing he went all the way home and washed them again, she still might not like them. However, if that is what she wanted, he would have to do that before he could get the Brownie book . . . and he started for the door.

"Well now, let's see what we can do," said the lady. "I know what," she said. "It's against the rules but perhaps we can wash them in here." And she led Rufus into a little room that smelled of paste where lots of new books and old books were stacked up. In one corner was a little round sink and Rufus washed his hands again. Then they returned to the desk. The lady got a chair and put a newspaper on it. She made Rufus stand on this because he was not big enough to write at the desk otherwise.

Then the lady put a piece of paper covered with a lot of printing in front of Rufus, dipped a pen in the ink well and gave it to him.

"All right," she said. "Here's your application. Write your name here."

All the writing Rufus had ever done before had been on big pieces of brown wrapping paper with lots of room on them. Rufus had often covered those great sheets of paper with his own kind of writing at home. Lines up and down.

But on this paper there wasn't much space. It was already covered with writing. However, there was a tiny little empty space and that was where Rufus must write his name, the lady said. So, little space or not, Rufus confidently grasped the pen with his left hand and dug it into the paper. He was not accustomed to pens, having always worked with pencils until now, and he made a great many holes and blots and scratches.

"Gracious," said the lady. "Don't bear down so hard! And why don't you hold it in your right hand?" she asked, moving the pen back into his right hand.

Rufus started again scraping his lines up and down and all over the page, this time using his right hand. Wherever there was an empty space he wrote. He even wrote over some of the print for good measure. Then he waited for the lady, who had gone off to get a book for some man, to come back and look.

"Oh," she said as she settled herself in her swivel chair, "is that the way you write? Well . . . it's nice, but what does it say?"

"Says Rufus Moffat. My name."

Apparently these lines up and down did not spell Rufus Moffat to this lady. She shook her head.

"It's nice," she repeated. "Very nice. But nobody but you knows what it says. You have to learn to write your name

better than that before you can join the library."

Rufus was silent. He had come to the library all by himself, gone back home to wash his hands, and come back because he wanted to take books home and read them the way the others did. He had worked hard. He did not like to think he might have to go home without a book.

The library lady looked at him a moment and then she said quickly before he could get himself all the way off the big chair, "Maybe you can *print* your name."

Rufus looked at her hopefully. He thought he could write better than he could print, for his writing certainly looked to him exactly like all grown people's writing. Still he'd try to print if that was what she wanted.

The lady printed some letters on the top of a piece of paper. "There," she said. "That's your name. Copy it ten times and then we'll try it on another application."

Rufus worked hard. He worked so hard the knuckles showed white on his brown fist. He worked for a long, long time, now with his right hand and now with his left. Sometimes a boy or a girl came in, looked over his shoulder and watched, but he paid no attention. From time to time the lady studied his work and she said, "That's fine. That's fine." At last she said, "Well, maybe now we can try." And she gave him another application.

All Rufus could get, with his large generous letters, in that tiny little space where he was supposed to print his name, was R-U-F. The other letters he scattered here and there on the card. The lady did not like this either. She gave him still another blank. Rufus tried to print smaller and this time he got RUFUS in the space, and also he crowded an M at the end. Since he was doing so well now the lady herself printed the *offat* part of Moffat on the next line.

"This will have to do," she said. "Now take this home and ask your mother to sign it on the other side. Bring it back on Thursday and you'll get your card."

Rufus's face was shiny and streaked with dirt where he had rubbed it. He never knew there was all this work to getting a book. The other Moffats just came in and got books. Well, maybe they had had to do this once too.

Rufus held his hard-earned application in one hand and steered his scooter with the other. When he reached home Joey, Jane and Sylvie were not around any longer. Mama signed his card for him, saying, "My! So you've learned how to write!"

"Print," corrected Rufus.

Mama kissed Rufus and he went back out. The lady had said to come back on Thursday, but he wanted a book today. When the other Moffats came home, he'd be sitting on the top step of the porch, reading. That would surprise them. He smiled to himself as he made his way to the library for the third time.

Once his application blew away. Fortunately it landed in a thistle bush and did not get very torn. The rest of the way Rufus clutched it carefully. He climbed the granite steps to the library again only to find that the big round dark brown doors were closed. Rufus tried to open them but he couldn't. He knocked at the door, even kicked it with his foot, but there was no answer. He pounded on the door but nobody came.

A big boy strode past with his newspapers. "Hey, kid," he said to Rufus. "Library's closed!" And off he went, whistling.

Rufus looked after him. The fellow said the library was closed. How could it have closed so fast? He had been here such a little while ago. The lady must still be here. He did want his Brownie book. If only he could see in, he might see the lady and get his book. The windows were high up but they had very wide sills. Rufus was a wonderful climber. He could shinny up trees and poles faster than anybody on the block. Faster than Joey. Now, helping himself up by means of one of the pine trees that grew close to the building, and by sticking his toes in the ivy and rough places in the bricks, he scrambled up the wall. He hoisted himself up on one of the sills and sat there. He peered in. It was dark inside, for the shades had been drawn almost all the way down.

"Library lady!" he called, and he knocked on the window-pane. There was no answer. He put his hands on each side of his face to shield his eyes, and he looked in for a long, long time. He could not believe that she had left. Rufus was resolved to get a book. He had lost track of the number of times he had been back and forth from home to the library, and the library home. Maybe the lady was in the cellar. He climbed down, stubbing his big toe on the bricks as he did so. He stooped down beside one of the low dirt-spattered cellar windows. He couldn't see in. He lay flat on the ground, wiped one spot clean on the window, picked up a few pieces of coal from the sill and put them in his pocket for Mama.

"Hey, lady," he called.

He gave the cellar window a little push. It wasn't locked so he opened it a little and looked in. All he could see was a high pile of coal reaching up to this window. Of course he didn't put any of that coal in his pocket for that would be stealing.

"Hey, lady," he yelled again. His voice echoed in the cellar but the library lady did not answer. He called out, "Hey, lady," every few seconds, but all that answered him was an echo. He pushed the window open a little wider. All of a sudden it swung wide open and Rufus slid in, right on top of the coal pile, and crash, clatter, bang! He slid to the bottom, making a great racket.

A little light shone through the dusty windows, but on the whole it was very dark and spooky down here and Rufus really wished that he was back on the outside looking in. However, since he was in the library, why not go upstairs quick, get the Brownie book, and go home? The window had banged shut, but he thought he could climb up the coal pile, pull the window up, and get out. He certainly hoped he could anyway. Supposing he couldn't and he had to stay in this cellar! Well, that he would not think about. He looked around in the dusky light and saw a staircase

across the cellar. Luckily his application was still good. It was torn and dirty but it still had his name on it, RUFUS M, and that was the important part. He'd leave this on the desk in exchange for the Brownie book.

Rufus cautiously made his way over to the steps but he

stopped halfway across the cellar. Somebody had opened the door at the top of the stairs. He couldn't see who it was, but he did see the light reflected and that's how he knew that somebody had opened the door. It must be the lady. He was just going to say, "Hey, lady," when he thought, "Gee, maybe it isn't the lady. Maybe it's a spooky thing."

Then the light went away, the door was closed, and Rufus was left in the dark again. He didn't like it down here. He started to go back to the coal pile to get out of this place. Then he felt of his application. What a lot of work he had done to get a book and now that he was this near to getting one, should he give up? No. Anyway, if it was the lady up there, he knew her and she knew him and neither one of them was scared of the other. And Mama always said there's no such thing as a spooky thing.

So Rufus bravely made his way again to the stairs. He tiptoed up them. The door at the head was not closed tightly. He pushed it open and found himself right in the library. But goodness! There in the little sink room right opposite him was the library lady!

Rufus stared at her in silence. The library lady was eating. Rufus had never seen her do anything before but play cards, punch books, and carry great piles of them around. Now she was eating. Mama said not to stare at anybody while they were eating. Still Rufus didn't know the library lady ate, so it was hard for him not to look at her.

She had a little gas stove in there. She could cook there. She was reading a book at the same time that she was eating. Sylvie could do that too. This lady did not see him.

"Hey, lady," said Rufus.

The librarian jumped up out of her seat. "Was that you in the cellar? I thought I heard somebody. Goodness, young man! I thought you had gone home long ago."

Rufus didn't say anything. He just stood there. He had gone home and he had come back lots of times. He had the whole thing in his mind; the coming and going, and going and coming, and sliding down the coal pile, but he did not know where to begin, how to tell it.

"Didn't you know the library is closed now?" she demanded, coming across the floor with firm steps.

Rufus remained silent. No, he hadn't known it. The fellow had told him but he hadn't believed him. Now he could see for himself that the library was closed so the library lady could eat. If the lady would let him take his

24

book, he'd go home and stay there. He'd play the game of Find the Duke with Jane. He hopefully held out his card with his name on it.

"Here this is," he said.

But the lady acted as though she didn't even see it. She led Rufus over to the door.

"All right now," she said. "Out with you!" But just as she opened the door the sound of water boiling over on the stove struck their ears, and back she raced to her little room.

"Gracious!" she exclaimed. "What a day!"

Before the door could close on him, Rufus followed her in and sat down on the edge of a chair. The lady thought he had gone and started to sip her tea. Rufus watched her quietly, waiting for her to finish.

After a while the lady brushed the crumbs off her lap. And then she washed her hands and the dishes in the little sink where Rufus had washed his hands. In a library a lady could eat and could wash. Maybe she slept here too. Maybe she lived here.

"Do you live here?" Rufus asked her.

"Mercy on us!" exclaimed the lady. "Where'd you come from? Didn't I send you home? No, I don't live here and neither do you. Come now, out with you, young man. I mean it." The lady called all boys "young man" and all girls "Susie." She came out of the little room and she opened the big brown door again. "There," she said. "Come back on Thursday."

Rufus's eyes filled up with tears.

"Here's this," he said again, holding up his application in a last desperate attempt. But the lady shook her head. Rufus went slowly down the steps, felt around in the bushes for his scooter, and with drooping spirits he mounted it. Then for the second time that day, the library lady changed her mind.

"Oh, well," she said, "come back here, young man. I'm not supposed to do business when the library's closed, but I see we'll have to make an exception."

So Rufus rubbed his sooty hands over his face, hid his scooter in the bushes again, climbed the granite steps and, without circling the light, he went back in and gave the lady his application.

The lady took it gingerly. "My, it's dirty," she said. "You really ought to sign another one."

"And go home with it?" asked Rufus. He really didn't

believe this was possible. He wiped his hot face on his sleeve and looked up at the lady in exhaustion. What he was thinking was: All right. If he had to sign another one, all right. But would she just please stay open until he got back?

However, this was not necessary. The lady said, "Well now, I'll try to clean this old one up. But remember, young man, always have everything clean—your hands, your book, everything, when you come to the library."

Rufus nodded solemnly. "My feet too," he assured her.

Then the lady made Rufus wash his hands again. They really were very bad this time, for he had been in a coal pile, and now at last she gave Rufus the book he wanted—one of the Palmer Cox Brownie books. This one was "The Brownies in the Philippines."

And Rufus went home.

When he reached home, he showed Mama his book. She smiled at him, and gave his cheek a pat. She thought it was fine that he had gone to the library and joined all by himself and taken out a book. And she thought it was fine when Rufus sat down at the kitchen table, was busy and quiet for a long, long time, and then showed her what he had done.

He had printed RUFUS M. That was what he had done. And that's the way he learned to sign his name. And that's the way he always did sign his name for a long, long time.

But, of course, that was before he ever went to school at all, when the Moffats still lived in the old house, the yellow house on New Dollar Street; before this country had gone into the war; and before Mr. Abbot, the curate, started leaving his overshoes on the Moffats' front porch.

2

A TRAINLOAD OF SOLDIERS

NOW THE MOFFATS LIVED IN A TINY LITTLE HOUSE SET far back from the street on Ashbellows Place. And Rufus could write and print the *offat* part of Moffat as well as Rufus M. He could do this with either hand, his right hand or his left hand. Moreover he was knitting a washcloth for the soldiers because now this country had joined the war. And Mr. Abbot, the young curate, left his overshoes more and more often on the Moffats' front porch as he thought up more and more reasons for coming to call. First it was cassocks Mama must sew for him. Then it was about the bazaar.

Of course, the real reason probably was that he hoped to find Sylvie at home. Maybe he hoped to marry her some day. All the Moffats thought this would not be surprising since she had the prettiest voice in the whole choir and did not sing fluttery like Mrs. Peale. So that was why Mr. Abbot's overshoes were on the porch so often. He always wore his overshoes in rain or shine because his work carried him far afield, through muddy fields and lots.

As for Sylvie, she was going to the Art School where she had won a scholarship. She was dancing and singing in every play that was put on for the soldiers. Moreover, she was working for the Red Cross. She was not knitting a washcloth, though. Rufus was.

Rufus was the only one of the four Moffats who was knitting a washcloth for the soldiers. Up in Jane's room at school they were knitting gray and khaki scarves and helmets. Even sweaters. And Jane was trying to learn how to purl. Not Rufus. You do not have to purl a washcloth. Just straight knit it.

Rufus's whole room was knitting washcloths. The teacher gave everybody a ball of string and showed them how to cast on. She usually explained all things twice to the class, once to the right-handers and once to Rufus, the only left-hander.

For some time Rufus had not been sure whether he was left-handed or right-handed. That was because his teachers had not been able to make up their minds, not till the teacher he had now, his Room Three teacher. It is true his Room One teacher considered him a left-handed boy and never tried to change him. But his Room Two teacher felt

it was her bounden duty at least to try to break Rufus of
the habit of writing with his left hand, even though he did
so much better with it than the right.

As a consequence Rufus's writing the year he was in
Room Two was very bad. Gold stars were awarded to those
children who wrote well, and according to the approved
Houston method. Rufus did not write well. Nevertheless
his Room Two teacher gave him gold stars because she
thought the great effort involved in writing with his right
hand merited the reward. Lest the class think that she was
rewarding him for that dreadful right-handed writing of
his, however, she always wrote in blue crayon along the top
of his paper, "Rufus did this with his *right* hand." It was
as though she would give a gold star to some right-handed
person who wrote with his left. But she hoped that by the
end of the year Rufus would be a good right-handed writer.

The teacher he had now, his Room Three teacher, decided that Rufus was definitely left-handed and he and the
world in general might as well get used to this fact. Rufus
was very happy to have the matter settled, because his left
hand had always seemed the right hand to him, the right
one that is for writing, eating, combing his hair, for pitch-

ing balls, playing marbles, and even mumblety-peg too.

At home Rufus had always been accepted as the only left-handed member of the family, and nobody had tried to switch him from left to right. He sat at the end of the table opposite Mama at dinner time. Since a left-handed eater's elbow is apt to bump into a right-handed eater's elbow, Rufus sat at the end of the table and bumped into no one.

And in school when the writing lesson was to begin and the children of Room Three were told to tilt their papers a little to the left, Rufus was told to tilt his a little to the right. The teacher hoped this would produce the same results all around. For a time this paper tilting was confusing to Rufus. He had a tendency to tip the paper practically upside down, encircle it with his left arm and write. After a while he learned to hold it at the proper angle and to cover it rapidly with those round spirals the teacher liked the class to make.

These spirals were not easy to make, left-handed or right-handed. Sylvie was the best spiral maker of the four Moffats. Her spirals began a certain size and ended the same size like one of her curls. Not Rufus's. His spirals grew larger and larger so that at the end of the line they covered twice as much space as at the beginning and looked like bed springs. But spirals were nothing compared to washcloths, and Rufus paid very close attention while the teacher showed how to cast on the stitches.

All the children cast the same number of stitches onto their needles, but this did not mean that all the washcloths were going to be the same size. Not at all. Some were big and some were small, although they all started out with the same number of stitches cast on.

Rufus's washcloth was one of the kind that grew wider and wider as it grew longer. He knit the way he wrote, with large loose generous stitches. And maybe it was because he was left-handed that many of his stitches had a way of turning upside down. Every now and then Jane cast off some stitches at the side for him so the washcloth would not become too wide. Also she added some stitches in the middle to fill in some of the biggest holes.

"Try and knit closer together," she urged Rufus. "This looks more like a fish net."

Sometimes in school, Room Three knit instead of doing their spelling or arithmetic. The girls went fast and the boys

went slow, but they all knit hard on their washcloths. One girl made three while Rufus made his one. This girl was Emma Ryder. She was sent from room to room with her washcloths. "Look!" said all the teachers to their classes. "A little girl in Room Three and she has made three washcloths!" And all the big girls who had not yet made three would squirm in their chairs and resolve to do better. Yes, she made three, but Rufus did work hard on his one and at last he finished it. In fact all the washcloths were finished now. Rufus's was very dirty, especially the beginning of it that he had knit the first. The end that he had just finished was not quite so dirty because the string inside the ball was still fairly clean.

Mama said she hoped she would be able to boil the dirt out of it and make it good and white for some soldier. Rufus watched her wash it and wash it. Finally it did get fairly white except for the first rows that Rufus had had to undo so many times in the beginning. These remained slightly gray. "But it's pure," said Mama, "because I boiled it."

Rufus then took it back to school. The teacher, Miss Wells, told the class to fold their washcloths and she passed around little squares of paper for them to print their names on and pin to their own washcloths.

Rufus M. Room Three, he printed. Of course he could have printed his whole name, but he had gotten in the habit of writing just M. for Moffat in the library that day long ago and he still signed his name that way.

Why did the teacher ask the class to sign their washcloths, Rufus wondered. Was there going to be a new place on their report cards marked "washcloths" where she would give them a good or a bad? Or, and this was more likely, he thought, did a soldier want to know who knit his washcloth so he could write a letter to the fellow who did? Rufus might get a letter some day from some soldier saying he liked this loose washcloth.

Two girls, Emma Ryder and another, then collected the washcloths and folded them in neat piles on the table in the front of the room. Rufus thought he could see his about half way down the outside pile. Because his was bigger than the others and the color more of a pearly gray, it was easy to recognize.

"There," said the teacher. "Now tomorrow I'll send them all over to the Red Cross and the Red Cross will send them overseas."

The class then sat with hands folded, hoping she would pass around another ball of string instead of the arithmetic books. But she didn't. She passed around the books.

Rufus was very happy to have finished his washcloth and now left-handed and right-handed washcloths alike were up there on the table and the soldiers would have them soon.

For a time Rufus was content with the thought that the Red Cross was going to take care of the matter of sending his washcloth overseas. He was content until that afternoon. Then the teacher said she had a surprise for them. The whole class, in fact the whole school, was going to march to the railroad station to wave good-by to a trainload of soldiers who were off to camp.

"Good," thought Rufus. "Here's a chance to give the washcloths to the soldiers right now. They won't have to wait until they get over there."

But the teacher did not think of that. She left the wash-cloths right where they were, and furthermore she told Rufus that she did not have time for questions now when he raised his hand to ask about this. "Girls in line," she said. "Boys in line." She did not mention washcloths. She only gave instructions. "Everybody stay in line all the way to the railroad station." Then she had the monitors pass around the flags and she gave the girls bouquets of flowers to toss to the soldiers.

The children stood in line in the hall. The lines stretched back into the cloakroom. All up and down the corridor other classes were lining up outside of their rooms. The youngest classes were to march out first, the highest last. Room One marched out now with Mr. Pennypepper, the Superintendent, leading in the very front. Room Two was warming up. "One, two. One, two," said the teacher.

Rufus's class would march out next. Rufus had become more and more bothered about the washcloths. Here they were, all of Room Three, marching to the station to see the soldiers off and they weren't taking the washcloths with them. This seemed foolish to Rufus. Why had they made these washcloths for the soldiers? For the soldiers to use, of course. The sooner they had them the better, he thought. It was funny the teacher didn't think of this.

"Ev-ry-bo-dy keep-in step, shoul-ders back, eyes a-head." That's what Miss Wells kept intoning and it was really all she seemed to have time to think about.

Rufus was sure that it was a mistake to leave the wash-cloths in the pile on the table. He guessed he'd go in and get his. He guessed he'd give it to a soldier himself this

afternoon. Quick! Before his class started moving! Now was a good chance because Miss Wells had stepped over to have a hurried word with the teacher of Room Four before giving the order to march. Rufus darted back into the classroom and over to the table where the washcloths for the soldiers were stacked. He pulled out one with a very dingy fringe along the edge. It looked familiar to him and he hoped it was his. It was! Hurrah! He stuffed it in his coat pocket.

As Rufus stepped back into his place in line, the teacher clapped her hands at him and shook her head disapprovingly, but that was all she did. And now he had his washcloth to give right to some soldier.

Room Three started to march out. The children marched straight down the long corridor and out the front door, not the side door children usually came in and out of, but the big front door. Ordinarily only Mr. Pennypepper and the important teachers used the big front door. The only time children were allowed to come in and go out this way was during fire drill, and occasionally if a child were sent to the Board of Health in the middle of the morning to see if he had the measles, he could use this door.

As Rufus's class marched down the granite steps, they could see Mr. Pennypepper leading the way all by himself at the head of Room One, and looking neither to the left nor the right, except at street corners when he held up his hand and made all traffic stop. But Rufus couldn't see Mr. Pennypepper any more once he had reached the sidewalk, except when he led the long column around the corners.

Now they were all marching down the street toward the railroad tracks. Rufus hoped they would march down under the bridge and up and out the other side. One thing he really loved to do was to be under the bridge when a train raced past on the tracks above. He liked to walk under the bridge anyway and smell the dampness, for there was usually a trickle of water oozing from the rough rock wall. If a train were not going past he could roar, himself, and fill the space up with a tremendous never-ending echo.

But Mr. Pennypepper did not lead the school down and under the bridge. He led the way up the gently sloping pebbly hill on this side of the tracks. Some of the children began to limp for they had cinders in their shoes. But they all kept in line. Even the big boys stayed where they were supposed to because the Superintendent, Pop Pennypepper, as he was affectionately called, was leading the procession.

Now Rufus's class started up the slope. Rufus could hear yelling up ahead. Soldiers probably. He patted his pocket and smiled. At any rate the soldiers would have one washcloth before they got over there. If the teacher had divided the pile of washcloths and said, "One half of these goes to the soldiers over there, and one half to the ones that have not left yet," why, that would be more fair, he thought. Well, anyway, they would have one—his. And this happy thought consoled Rufus for the disappointment over not marching under the bridge.

A pebble went through the hole in the bottom of Rufus's shoe and lodged between the layers of leather. He had to walk on his heel. But he didn't think about that. There were the soldiers! All dressed in khaki! A whole trainload of them, yelling and waving their hats and leaning far out of the windows to catch the flowers and shake hands!

All the classes took turns going to the train. First Room One and then Room Two. The little girls were tossing their flowers everywhere—at the soldiers, through the windows, and on the train itself. Rufus stamped up and down impatiently. He could see that when Room Three pressed ahead to the train he could easily give a soldier his washcloth.

He grinned when he thought how surprised the soldier would be. Here the soldiers were, all getting plenty of asters and chrysanthemums, but not one single washcloth so far. As it happened, thought Rufus, wiping his sweaty hand on it, it was good his had turned out to be a big loose one like a fish net, rather than a small tight one like Emma Ryder's. It would go farther.

"Hurry up, Room Two. Get out of the way," he yelled. Nobody could hear him because everybody else was yelling. At last Miss Wells clapped her hands. "All right, Room Three," she said. And boys and girls rushed to the train.

Rufus clutched his washcloth in his fist, not realizing that he was getting it all smudged again. It was good that Mama could not see it now. It still had his name, Rufus M.

Room Three, pinned to it. Rufus did not think to take this off. The teacher had said to put it on, so he left it on.

The boys were waving flags. The girls were throwing flowers. The soldiers were catching them and putting them in their buttonholes, behind their ears, and in their hats. And Rufus was looking for the captain. All the soldiers looked like captains to him. He shook hands with a lot of them and one soldier whisked him up and stood him on the platform. Rufus felt like a soldier himself and in the excitement he forgot about his washcloth. He had it in his hand but he forgot to give it to anybody. Maybe it was because it was in his left hand and everybody was shaking his right. Anyway, when the teacher said, "All right now, Room Three, step back into place," Rufus still had his washcloth in his hand and he still did not remember about it.

He did not remember until Room Three was all lined up across the way again. Then, "Criminenty!" exclaimed Rufus. "I forgot the washcloth!" And before anyone could stop him he bolted out of line and ran back to the train. Nobody was at the train at this moment. Room Three had left it and Room Four was about to come. Only Rufus was at the train. All the soldiers were grinning at him and watching him. The whole school was watching him, in fact. Mr. Pennypepper was rocking from heel to toe.

Many little girls looked from Rufus to Mr. Pennypepper wondering what he would do. And the boys asked themselves, "Did Rufus have a special part to play in this performance?" And Miss Wells clapped helplessly. To have Rufus alone at the train was not part of the program. But Rufus was not thinking about this. He was only thinking now about what soldier he should give his washcloth to. He wished he had been as good a knitter as Emma Ryder who held the record for Room Three and in the end had made six! None of the six was as big as his, though.

There was one curly-haired soldier leaning out the window, chewing gum and cheering lustily. Rufus thought he looked sort of like the one who had hoisted him onto the platform. He wore his khaki hat way back on his head and it was a wonder it did not fall off. He was a real husky soldier. Rufus reached his hand up and pressed his washcloth into the soldier's large palm.

"Here," yelled Rufus. "You want it? It's a washcloth."

The soldier's fist closed on it. "Ouch!" he said. "What bit me?"

"Oh," warned Rufus, too late. "Look out for the pin. It's just my name."

"And is this for me?" asked the soldier, holding the washcloth up.

"Yeh. I made it. I knitted it," explained Rufus.

"Gee, thanks!" said the soldier, and he mopped his face with it and gave Rufus a broad grin and a wink.

Rufus smiled. He forgot he was supposed to be in line with Room Three. He did not know that everybody was watching him, including Mr. Pennypepper, and he started to back down the slope, thinking he'd go home now that he'd delivered his washcloth.

His teacher thought differently. "Rufus Moffat, come back here," she called.

But Rufus did not hear her because all the soldiers were having a good time cheering him and he had to wave back. Mr. Pennypepper, who had been holding Room Four at bay until Rufus should be out of the way, and who had been rocking back and forth on his toes, and jingling the keys in his pocket through all this interruption in the plans, hurried after Rufus himself and turned him around.

"Criminenty!" exclaimed Rufus when he saw Mr. Pen-

nypepper, and he tore back to his place in line midst more loud cheers from the soldiers.

All of this inspired Mr. Pennypepper to make a little speech. He stood on the platform beside the train and, turning now to the soldiers and now to the children of the school, he said that this one washcloth was a symbol. It was a symbol representing how the people of Cranbury were behind our soldiers in the great combat overseas.

When the cheering that greeted Mr. Pennypepper's impromptu speech subsided, Room Four proceeded with the regular program. From then on everything went according to schedule. Nobody else had brought washcloths. Just asters and chrysanthemums. Finally the whole school sang songs, and at last the train began to move slowly, slowly, down the tracks.

Rufus happened to be standing near a telegraph pole. He quickly shinnied up it to see if he could see his soldier. There he was! And he saw Rufus too! He mopped his face again with the washcloth and pointed to his chest. Rufus saw that he had pinned his name, Rufus M., to his khaki coat. Rufus laughed. This was some soldier! The train began to gather momentum now. Faster and faster it went, but Rufus's soldier hung way out of the window and waved his washcloth as long as you could see anything, until the train disappeared down the tracks and across the marsh.

"Good-by, soldier!" yelled Rufus, and he slid down the pole.

Mr. Pennypepper started leading the classes back down the hill and away from the railroad station. All the children marched as far as Elm Street and there they were dismissed.

Rufus went straight home. He looked around for some string. He found some wound up in a ball in the pantry. It was red string. This would make a good washcloth, he thought, for he intended to make another one. Of course he couldn't cast on. But Jane did that for him.

"What's this gonna be?" she asked.

"Washcloth," said Rufus. "A red one."

But Rufus did not have enough red string to make a whole washcloth, only enough for two or three rows. He did find some blue and some white string and he wondered how it would be to make a red, white, and blue washcloth. Nobody could tell him. "Try it," they said. So every now and then he knit a row of white and then a row of blue.

The trouble with this washcloth was that it had knots in it where he joined the red to the blue.

"You should learn to splice," said Joey, who could splice rope. But before Rufus finished his red, white, and blue washcloth, one day the postman came right into Room Three.

"Is there a Rufus M. in this room?" he demanded, looking over his glasses at the class.

"Yes," yelled the whole class, pointing to Rufus.

"Here's mail for him," said the postman. And he handed Rufus a postcard.

Rufus was stunned. At first he could not move. The only time he had ever gotten a postcard before in his life was from Sylvie when she went away to Camp Lincoln for a week. And on Valentine's Day he got valentines but not from the letterman. They came under the door with a ring of the bell and stamping of feet on the porch. Come to think of it nobody ever got letters right in school. Home was where letters came, if there were letters. At last he managed to stand up and go to the front of the room and take his postcard. He examined it a long time It had a picture of a soldier laughing on it. He turned it over. It was addressed to Rufus M., Room Three, School, Cranbury, Conn., U.S.A. The message on it was this:

"The washcloth you knitted sure comes in handy. My buddies and I all take turns. Al."

Al—that was that soldier's name. Rufus smiled. He showed it to everybody and then he put it in his pocket and he kept it there always.

3

THE INVISIBLE PIANO PLAYER

RUFUS DID NOT THINK ABOUT THE INVISIBLE PIANO PLAYER all the time. He ate, drank, slept, went to school, went to Sunday School, read his postcard from the soldier, Al, hiked up East Rock with Joey, and played, most of the time. Still, whenever he went past a certain house on Pleasant Street, he did think about the invisible piano player who lived there.

The Saybolts lived in this house; Mr. Saybolt, a motorman on the Bridgeport Express, and Mrs. Saybolt, his wife. She called all children "Tigers!" and chased them off her white sidewalk and out of her hedge chairs—two hedges in front of the porch she kept clipped in the shape of armchairs. She was a jolly lady on the whole, who sometimes laughed and talked to herself when she was hanging up the clothes. She just did not want children sitting in her hedge chairs. Rufus did not know whether the invisible piano player was named Saybolt or not. He had never seen him. So far as he knew neither had anybody else ever seen him. This was natural since he was invisible.

It happened quite by accident that Rufus found out about the invisible piano player. Nobody told Rufus a word about him in advance.

One day Mama sent Rufus to the Saybolts' house with Mrs. Saybolt's new navy blue dress. It was not far, just around the corner. But Rufus was proud to go there with the new navy blue dress because it was the first time that Mama had ever let him deliver any of her dressmaking

alone. That meant he was a big fellow in the family now.

Rufus walked up on Mrs. Saybolt's porch. She wouldn't call him "Tiger," because he was here on business. Inside someone was playing the piano. Rufus rang the bell. Nobody answered the door. He rang again. Still no one answered. They couldn't all be out because somebody was playing the piano. Rufus supposed no one could hear the bell because the person playing the piano was making so much noise. The door was open, so Rufus stepped in. He stood for a moment in the hall.

"Hey," he called in a lull in the music.

Nobody came. And the music began again, so Rufus stepped into the parlor expecting to see Mrs. Saybolt playing. Then he stood transfixed in the doorway. There was music coming from the piano. The keys were hopping up and down, playing a lively tune. But, *nobody was sitting at the piano playing it.*

Rufus recognized in a flash what it was—an invisible piano player!

Rufus stood there, watching. He knew about invisible people. Certain people who wore certain cloaks were invisible. Jane had read him a story only this morning about one of these fellows. That one happened to be a prince, an invisible prince.

Rufus would have liked to stay there forever watching the invisible piano player, but just then Mrs. Saybolt came downstairs, scooped up her navy blue dress, pinned three dollars to a piece of paper, gave it to Rufus, and scooped him out the door, dropping two cents in his palm for himself. He didn't have a chance to ask one word about the fellow.

That was the first time that Rufus knew about the invisible piano player. But always after that when Rufus went past this house he thought about him, especially if he could hear him busy at the piano. When he wasn't playing the piano, Rufus wondered if he sat in the hedge chairs. He could sit there because Mrs. Saybolt could not see him. He wondered many things about the man. He wondered if you could feel an invisible man or if touching him would be like touching air. He asked Jane.

Jane thought a long time. Then she said she thought you could feel an invisible man. The only thing you couldn't do

was see him. If he sneezed or coughed, she thought you could hear him. Hear him and feel him, that's what she thought.

This sounded sensible to Rufus. He wished Mama would send him to the Saybolts' house again, but right now Mama was not sewing for Mrs. Saybolt. Rufus hoped that some day he'd have a chance to go back to this house and look at the stool where the invisible piano player sat. Then he would try to touch him and really find out if you can feel an invisible man or not.

Going to school and coming home from school Rufus passed the Saybolts' house. Whenever he heard the invisible piano player, he paused to listen. This was the only invisible man he knew about outside of those fellows in books. And he was a smart man. To be invisible is smart in itself. But to be invisible and such a good piano player also was quite remarkable. "A Paderooski," thought Rufus. This chap never missed a beat. Tum-te-tum! He never struck the wrong note, the way he and Jane did on their organ. He never had to practice exercises either, the way Nancy Stokes did. He just played. Rufus admired him very much.

Rufus listened from outside and across the street as much

as he could. But the opportunity to get inside the house again did not present itself for a long time. Then one day when he heard the invisible piano player he stopped to listen for a moment. He could hear him very well because the window on the porch was open. Mrs. Saybolt was nowhere in sight. So Rufus tiptoed up on the porch and looked through the open window. This was almost as good as being inside the house. And there was the invisible piano player as invisible as ever!

Rufus watched the keys hop up and down and he tried to imagine what the invisible piano player might look like if he didn't have his cloak of invisibility on.

All the while that Rufus was watching through the window he kept one ear cocked for Mrs. Saybolt, so he could run if she came and called him "Tiger!"

Then it occurred to Rufus that perhaps the reason the piano player stayed invisible was that he might be afraid of Mrs. Saybolt. In that case the invisible piano player might not be a man after all. He might be a boy like Rufus. He might be a boy who did not like to be called "Tiger!" and therefore made himself invisible.

"Are you scared of Mrs. Saybolt?" he asked. "Don't he

63

scared. I won't let her hurt you."

At this moment Mrs. Saybolt came around the corner of the house, her apron full of twigs she had snapped off the hedge. "Shoo, tiger!" she shouted.

Rufus tore home and crawled into the little old chicken coop where he thought for a while. But he couldn't stay there long because curiosity won the upper hand. He must find out once and for all: Can you feel an invisible man or is he like thin air?

With bits of feathers and chicken dirt clinging to him, he returned to the home of the invisible piano player. Mrs. Saybolt was in the back yard now, her mouth full of clothespins, hanging up the laundry. She did not see Rufus.

Rufus decided to hop in the open window, feel the place where the piano player should be, and then hop out. He stepped over the low window sill into the parlor. But he didn't go right over and touch the invisible person. He suddenly felt shy about that. He couldn't see the invisible man but the invisible man could probably see him and would not want him to get too close while he was playing. Rufus sat down on the edge of a chair and watched.

Up and down, up and down, hopped the keys. *Clinkety-*

clinkety! Poompty-poomp!

There came a little pause in the music.

"Hey, mister," said Rufus, in case it were a man and not a boy after all.

Nobody answered him. The music began again. This piano player was wonderful. *Poompty-poomp!* Rufus stared hard, watching the keys hop up and down all along the keyboard from one end to the other. At last Rufus stood up. He cautiously approached the piano. Now he was going to touch the invisible piano player's hand, if possible.

Rufus reached out his chubby fist. The keys kept hopping up and down very fast and Rufus swooped his hand up and down the keyboard but he did not feel anybody's hand there. It was a very scary thing to do, feeling for an invisible piano player's hands.

"I see you, fella," said Rufus to reassure himself. Since there was no answer to this remark, only that same uncanny hopping up and down of the keys, Rufus began to feel bolder. He tapped where he supposed a shoulder would be if a man were sitting there. He felt nothing. He quickly touched the stool, ran his chubby hand all over it. He still felt nothing. Rufus's spine tingled with excitement He retreated across the room and stood under a big rubber plant. He had put his hand right through an invisible man! That was proof all right. An invisible man cannot be felt! He cannot be seen and he cannot be felt! He is like thin air and

you can walk right through him or hundreds like him and never even know it.

Wait till he told Jane that! All the time she was going around thinking an invisible person can be felt. "That's not so. What would be the advantage anyway of being invisible if people bumped into you all the time," Rufus thought in disgust.

Poompety, poompety! From beneath the rubber plant Rufus watched the invisible musician, thinking of the hands that were making the keys hop up and down so fast, never forgetting a note. "A Paderooski all right," thought Rufus. "An invisible Paderooski," and he imagined him tossing his hair off his forehead.

All of a sudden in rushed Mrs. Saybolt. She dashed over to the piano and then she dashed out of the room again, fortunately without seeing Rufus. But when she left, the invisible man began to play faster. Goodness, how fast he went! Rufus got dizzy watching the keys pop up and down.

Then Mrs. Saybolt raced back into the room. Rufus guessed she did not like the fast way the invisible man was playing. Rufus could not see what she did to him, perhaps she rapped his knuckles, but when she left this time, the man (Rufus decided it must be a man; no boy could play that fast) began to play very slowly. *Poo-oomp-ty, poo-mp.* Instead of pelting down like raindrops, the keys rose and sank so slowly you would almost think there was another invisible man inside the piano trying to hold the notes back.

"Play slow too, don't you?" said Rufus, ruminating on this.

Once he had gone to the moving pictures. He had seen pictures of athletes racing and of a ballgame. Then they did tricks with the movie. They made it go lickety-cut. The racers looked as though they were running right out of the screen at you and you couldn't help ducking so they wouldn't step on you. Then they made the movie run very slowly. The runners looked as though they could scarcely pick up their feet, as though they were made of lead. And then they made the movie go backwards. The runners were whisked back to their starting point, and in the baseball game the ball was sucked right back into the pitcher's mitt. It was quite miraculous.

Now this invisible piano player was going so slowly that maybe the next thing he would do would be to play backwards. He had played fast and he had played slow; also just right. But would he play backwards, Rufus wondered. Could he?

"Hey, fella," he said cautiously. "Could you play 'My Country 'Tis of Thee' backwards?"

Then he felt ashamed of himself for asking such a question. How did he know this man could play "My Country 'Tis of Thee" forwards, let alone backwards. Just because

he, Rufus, could play "My Country 'Tis of Thee" frontwards very fast on the Moffats' little organ did not mean that everybody else could play that song too. And he himself had never tried it backwards.

But this man was such a remarkable player! Rufus imagined that he could easily play backwards as well as fast, slow, and just right.

Poompety, poomp! The invisible piano player struck the last note. He had finished what he was playing. Maybe he was tired now. Maybe that was why he was playing so slowly. The keys were still. There was silence for a moment and Rufus strained his eyes, hoping to see just the vaguest outline of the invisible man.

Then Rufus jumped! There was a sudden rattling noise inside the piano and a little slot above the keys sprang open, revealing the inner workings of the piano. Then came more rattling sounds and some round thing kept winding rapidly.

"He's going inside where the machinery is, that's what!" thought Rufus excitedly.

"Hey, is that your house, mister?" he asked.

There was no answer to this question.

"Might be a boy after all," thought Rufus, "because that

hole is not very big. Might be about my size," he thought.

Rufus waited to see if the invisible piano player would come out and play again. But the keys remained still. No more hopping up and down. The man was through. And at this moment Rufus heard Mrs. Saybolt coming. He ran out of the door as fast as he could, leaving the astonished Mrs. Saybolt standing in the hall shouting "Tiger!"

"Wanted to hear the player," Rufus called back as he ran down the street.

He tore home. He ran around to the back yard and crawled into the little chicken coop again to think about the invisible piano player. A man like that might be able to get through key holes.

"Criminenty!" exclaimed Rufus aloud, at this thought.

Speaking out loud revealed his whereabouts to Joey who had come to look for him.

"Hey, Rufe," he said, "get your wagon. Just saw Mrs. Saybolt and she said we could have that big box that her new player piano came in."

"She did!" said Rufus. And he added, "Did she say we could have him too?"

Through Rufus's mind flashed the vision of life in the

Moffats' house if they had an invisible person there too. Where would he sleep? There were no extra beds. Just enough beds. He could sleep on the yellow couch maybe.

On the other hand he might not need a bed at all. He could sleep in the air.

A chap like that in the house would not be an altogether pleasant addition to the family. For instance, he could eat all the dinner off their plates and they wouldn't even see him doing it. If he ate as fast as he played the piano, there would be nothing left for the Moffats. Since he couldn't be felt, they couldn't grab hold of his wrist and stop him. Mama would have to divide the butter into six parts, and even at that how could they explain to him that in this house it was share and share alike? So Rufus was really quite relieved when Joe answered absent-mindedly:

"Who? Said we could have the box, that's all. Good box."

"Yeh," said Rufus, crawling out of the chicken coop. "That might be where he sleeps though, and where's he gonna sleep if we take that away?"

"Who sleeps in that box?" asked Joe in disgust. "Nobody'd want to sleep in that old box."

Now this was just the kind of a box that Rufus felt he would really like to sleep in himself. He could fix it up and have it for his own house. So he was really glad to know that the invisible piano player did not sleep in it. He probably did sleep inside the piano with the machinery after all. Rufus got his express wagon and he and Joey went down Pleasant Street to Mrs. Saybolt's. While they were hoisting the big wooden crate sideways onto Rufus's wagon and trying to balance it there, Mrs. Saybolt came out to lend a hand. Rufus and Joey did not run because she had asked them here.

"And this is the lad who loves music," she said in a deep hearty voice. She really was not bad close to. She just didn't want people trying to sit in her hedge chairs. "Yes," she repeated, "it's a pleasure to see a boy his age who likes music that much," and she fastened her eyes on Rufus. "Before you go now, come in and hear my player piano for a while."

Rufus looked at Joey. Mrs. Saybolt was inviting them into her house to hear the invisible piano player! He glowed. Joey did not look so happy at the thought. Today was his day for dusting the pews. But who could say no to Mrs. Saybolt? Since ordinarily she chased you away, yelling "Tiger!" after you, when she wanted to be nice you had to be nice to her. That's the way Joey figured anyway, so he and Rufus went indoors.

Mrs. Saybolt preceded them, and Rufus observed that she had already told the invisible piano player to play. He was slightly disappointed, because he thought this time he might have seen the fellow hop out of his house with part of his cloak not on him. Then Rufus might have seen an arm or a leg. But no, the fellow was already playing by the time Joey and Rufus entered the parlor. *Poomp-ty, poomp!*

Mrs. Saybolt had a davenport instead of a couch or a sofa and Joey and Rufus sat on this. Mrs. Saybolt stood beside the piano and watched Rufus with an amiable smile.

"Plays nice, doesn't it?"

"It!" thought Rufus.

"Sure does," agreed Joey.

"Now I'll play a march," she said. She pushed a button, opened a little hole over the piano, took out a roll, put another in, and pushed another valve. The music began again. *Rat-ta-tat! Boom! Boom!*

Rufus looked at this proceeding with unbelieving eyes. The invisible piano player had been very real to him. And now instead of there being an invisible piano player the thing worked by machinery! Rufus felt cheated.

"Criminenty!" he exclaimed in disgust. "It's a machine. It's not an invisible piano player! Come on!" he said to Joe. "Let's go!"

He tore out of the house and Joey followed him, giving Mrs. Saybolt an apologetic wave of the arm. They got their box and their wagon and teetered home with it, planning what they would do with such a good crate.

Mrs. Saybolt never could get Rufus to come in and listen to her player piano again. She coaxed him with cookies for a while. Then she gave up. She decided she must have made a mistake about Rufus loving music so much. She soon fell into the habit of calling him "Tiger!" again and chasing him off her white sidewalk.

As for Rufus, every time he went past that house and heard the piano playing his pulse beat very rapidly for a second as he thought of the invisible piano player, and then it calmed down completely when he reminded himself, "Oh, a machine!"

4

RUFUS AND THE FATAL FOUR

USUALLY IT MADE NO DIFFERENCE WHETHER OR NOT RUFUS was a left-handed person. In fact, now that the teacher had accepted this quirk in Rufus's make-up, it was only awkward to be left-handed when somebody wanted to shake his right hand. So far no left-handed person had tried to shake hands with Rufus. Rufus hoped to meet one some day and then they would have a good left-handed shake.

But there was one occasion when it really was an asset to be left-handed, Rufus found. And that was in connection with the Fatal Four.

For some time Rufus had been seeing "The F. F." on all of Janey's notebooks and on the brown covers of her grammar and arithmetic books. He asked Jane what it meant. Jane said it was a secret. However, if Rufus would not tell anybody, the initials stood for the Fatal Four. More than that she would not say. Rufus assumed it had something to do with pirates. Therefore he was really surprised when Jane, in a mood of confidence, further enlightened him to the extent of revealing that the Fatal Four was the name of a baseball team she belonged to that could beat anybody.

"Then," she went on to explain, "if the Fatal Four gets tired of baseball, oh, not gets tired 'cause they'll never do that, but if it should snow, and they couldn't play any more, they'll still be the Fatal Four because it's a good name the members can keep always. Baseball . . . football . . . no matter what. Or it could just be a club to eat cookies and drink punch made out of jelly and water."

This all sounded good to Rufus, particularly the punch. He asked if he could join. Did it cost anything? Jane said she was sorry but the Fatal Four was all girls. However, she would try to bring him a cookie if they ever decided on punch and cookies instead of baseball. So for a time Rufus was not allowed to have anything to do with this team. But sometimes he went across the street to the big empty lot behind the library, sat down on a log, and watched them practice. There were a half-dozen or so silvery gray old telephone poles piled up in one part of the lot. Bleachers, Rufus called them, and that was where he sat to watch the Fatal Four.

Jane and Nancy had organized the Fatal Four baseball team. At first Jane was worried that they were playing baseball in October when the time for baseball is spring. She thought it would be better if the Fatal Four started right in with punch and cookies on Tuesdays. But once they had begun playing baseball she wondered how she could ever have been so foolish. She loved baseball and could not understand how anybody was happy who did not play it every day.

Naturally, since Jane and Nancy had thought up this whole team, there was no reason why they should not take the two most important roles, the pitcher and the catcher, for themselves. Jane was the catcher. She accepted this position because she thought the name alone would automatically make her a good one. "Yes," she said, "I'll be catcher." And she put her trust in the power of the title and the mitt to enable her to catch anything. Nancy was the pitcher. For a time they were the only members of the team, so they had to be the pitcher and the catcher, for in baseball that is the very least you can get along with. Soon, however, other girls in the neighborhood joined up.

"I'll be the captain," said Nancy. "Let's take a vote."

They took a vote and elected Nancy. Clara Pringle was the outfield to catch all flies. She never really had very much to do because there weren't many flies hit and she sat in the long grass and waited for business. A girl named Hattie Wood was first base. That made four girls they had on the team and that was when they decided to call themselves the Fatal Four.

So far Rufus had had nothing to do with this team except to sit and watch. He did this gladly however, for he considered that anything that called itself the Fatal Four was worthy of being watched, especially if there was that vague possibility of pink punch and cookies in the offing.

He used to sit there pounding his fist into one of Joey's old mitts, hoping they'd take him into the Four.

At first the Fatal Four baseball team practiced ardently every day. However, after a week or so Jane grew tired of chasing balls, since she rarely caught one. The mitt and the title of catcher had not produced the desired results.

"A back-stop is what we need," she told Nancy.

None of the girls was willing to be a back-stop. Moreover, they were all needed where they were. Take Hattie Wood off first base and what kind of a team would they have, they asked themselves. An amateur team. The Fatal Four was anything but that, Nancy assured them. "But if you want a back-stop, why not ask Rufus?" she suggested.

Now there was much arguing back and forth as to whether or not they should invite Rufus to be the back-stop. He was not a girl and this team was supposed to be composed of girls only. But then everybody thought how nice it would be to have Rufus chasing balls for them, so they enthusiastically assented.

"After all," said Jane, "a back-stop is not really part of the team. It's part of the grounds."

So that clinched it and that was how Rufus came to be

back-stop for the Fatal Four baseball team. Rufus was happy over the arrangement. When they abandoned baseball for punch and cookies, he might be an accepted member. Moreover, the more practice he had, the sooner the big boys would take him into their team, he thought. Certainly if the pitcher of the boys' baseball team had the same tendencies as Nancy, left-handed Rufus would be a tremendous asset.

Nancy used to be a rather good pitcher. But ever since the girls' baseball team had been organized, Nancy had taken to practicing curves. Somehow these curves always shot the ball way to the left of the batter. The batter would move farther and farther to the left, hoping to catch up with Nancy's curves. But it was no use. No matter how far to the left the batter edged, the farther to the left flew Nancy's balls. Often the bases had to be moved several times during the game to catch up with the home plate. Frequently, by the end of the game, home plate was where the pitcher's box originally had been, and vice versa. Nancy realized there was a flaw in her pitching which she would have to correct.

Meanwhile, it certainly was lucky the team now had a

left-handed back-stop, for Jane had a hard enough time catching just straight pitches, let alone these curves of Nancy's that veered off to the left all the time. But Rufus had only to reach out his left arm farther and farther, and he caught most of them. What he didn't catch he cheerfully ran for, over Mr. Buckle's hen coop or in Mrs. Wood's asparagus patch that had gone to seed, or he hunted between the long silvery logs that lay lined up in a corner of the field.

As a reward for his back-stop duties Nancy pitched Rufus some curves, and since he was a left-handed batter, her balls that veered to the left were just perfect for him and it was only when Rufus was at the bat that Clara Pringle, picking goldenrod in the outfield, had anything to do in the game.

This convinced Nancy that there was nothing wrong with her pitching after all. The trouble lay with the material she was working with. "Slug at 'em, fellas," she said. "Rufe hits 'em all." And the girls, feeling rather ashamed, now tried harder, sometimes even turning around and batting left-handed as Rufus did, hoping to hit Nancy's balls.

One Saturday morning Rufus was sitting in the driver's seat of the old abandoned sleigh that was in the Moffats'

barn. He was thinking that if he had a pony next winter he could harness it to this old sleigh and go for a ride. Suddenly Nancy and Janey burst around from the front yard. Nancy was swinging her bat. She had her pitcher's mitt on. Jane was pounding the baseball into Joey's big catcher's mitt, limbering it up.

"Come on, Rufe," they yelled. "This is *the* day!"

"What! Punch and cookies?" exclaimed Rufus.

"No, we're having a real game today. Not just practice," they said.

For a long time Jane and Nancy had thought they were the only girls' baseball team in Cranbury, in the world in fact. Then one day a girl accosted them after school. She said her name was Joyce Allen and that she was the captain of the Busy Bee baseball team, a team composed entirely of girls on the other side of town. She wanted to know whether or not Nancy, the captain of the F. F. team, would accept a challenge from her, the captain of the Busy Bee team, to play next Saturday. Nancy consulted with Jane and said "Yes."

So now today was the day. Rufus climbed off the sleigh, found his old pitcher's mitt that he used to catch Nancy's curves, and they all marched across the street to the big lot behind the library where the game was going to be held. While they waited for the teams to show up, Rufus spit in his mitt, rubbed sand in it, and got it into condition to play.

"I hope we don't have to go all over town and round everybody up," said Jane impatiently.

The Fatal Four had added another team member, Nancy's sister Beatrice, but they still called themselves the Fatal Four because it sounded better than fatal anything else. Since this team had such an excellent name, the F. F., it had plenty of applicants to join. Nancy and Jane were particular, however, saying to join the F. F. you really had to know something about baseball. Most applicants backed away apologetically when Nancy stated this firmly.

At last here came somebody across the lot. It was Joyce Allen, the captain of the Busy Bees.

"The others will be here soon," she said cheerfully. "Some of them hadn't finished washing the breakfast dishes, but they'll be here soon."

"While we're waitin'," said Jane, "since both the captains are here, we can see who's up at the bat first."

Rufus took the bat, threw it, and Nancy caught it. She

put her right fist around the end of it, then the other captain put her fist above Nancy's and swiftly placing one fist above the other they measured the length of the bat. The

visiting captain's left fist was the last one to fit the bat. It was a tight squeeze but fair, and Rufus said that the visiting team was first up at the bat. Rufus sometimes had to act in the capacity of umpire as well as back-stop.

But where was the visiting team? Or Nancy's, for that matter?

Rufus began to feel impatient. Here were the captains. All right. Let the teams come then. "Why not have the punch instead?" he asked. But nobody paid any attention to him. It seemed to Rufus as though the game were off, and he decided, Fatal Four or no, to go and find something else to do. Over in a corner of the field some men had started to dig a cellar to a new house. This activity looked interesting to Rufus and he was about to investigate it when along came two girls, arms linked together. So Rufus stayed. There was always the possibility that the Fatal Four might switch from baseball to punch and cookies. Either was worth staying for in Rufus's opinion.

"These girls must be Busy Bees," said Nancy.

They *were* Busy Bees. They both admitted it. However, they said they wished they could join the F. F. instead. They liked the name of it. They had heard many rumors as to what it stood for. Most people thought it stood for Funny Fellows. Did it?

"Of course not!" said Nancy, and Jane clapped her hand over Rufus's mouth before he could say the Fatal Four and give away the secret. No matter what it stood for, the girls wanted to join it and be able to write the F. F. on all their red notebooks.

While the discussion was going on three more girls arrived, three more Busy Bees. It seemed they too wanted to join the F. F., so they could write the F. F. on their notebooks also. Nancy and Jane looked at the captain. She must feel very badly at this desertion. But she didn't. She said she wished she could join the F. F. too.

"Oh, no," said Nancy. "You all better stay Busy Bees. What team would there be for us to beat if we let you join ours?"

So that settled the matter and Busy Bees remained Busy Bees. Now they lined up at the home plate for they were to be the first at the bat. At last the game began. "Thank goodness, Rufus is here behind me," thought Jane, pounding her fist into the big catcher's mitt. For it really took two Moffats to make one good catcher. If one of them was she, that is.

Nancy's team did not get off to a good start. Nancy had been practicing her curves more than ever, and they swung more and more sharply to the left. If they had not had such a good left-handed back-stop as Rufus, goodness knows where the balls would have landed. In order that they would not crash through a window of the library, the girls rearranged the bases many times.

Of course there was no danger of the balls crashing through the library windows from hits. The danger lay in Nancy's curves. So far she had not been able to strike the Busy Bees out. They were all walking to base on balls. And the balls were flying wild now. Rufus had dashed across the lot to take a look at the men who were digging the cellar to the new house and he was sorely missed. Jane, who had had enough trouble catching in the old days before Nancy cultivated her curves, was becoming desperate.

Right now happened to be a very tense moment. The captain of the Busy Bees was at the bat. There were men on all bases. They'd gotten there on walks. The captain had two strikes against her, however. She had been striking at anything, for she evidently had grown tired of just walking to base. If Nancy could strike her out, it would break the charm and maybe the Fatal Four team would have a chance at the bat. So far the Busy Bees had been at the bat the entire game. The score must be big. They had lost track of it.

Beside wanting to strike Captain Allen out, Nancy was

trying especially hard to impress her. She came over to Jane and said in a low voice, "They'll think they have a better team than we have, and I bet that pitcher can't even throw curves! I've just got to strike her out!"

"Yes," agreed Jane, who was anxious to bat herself for a change.

"Watch for a certain signal," Nancy said. "When I hold my two middle fingers up, it means I'm going to throw a curve, a real one. It'll curve out there by the library, and then it will veer back, right plunk over the home plate. She won't strike at it because she'll think it's going over the library. But it won't, and she'll miss it and that's the way I'll put her out."

Jane nodded her head. Another curve! Of course curves made it real baseball and not amateur. She knew that much. All the same she wished she had said, "Why don't you pitch 'em straight for a change?" But she didn't have the courage. Nancy was the captain and the pitcher. She certainly should know how to pitch if she was the pitcher. Nancy wasn't telling Jane how to catch. She expected Jane to know how to catch since she was the catcher. She didn't tell her anything. So neither did Jane tell Nancy anything.

and she waited for the signal and wished that Rufus would return and back-stop for this very important pitch.

Now Nancy was winding her arm around and around. Then she stopped. She held up her middle two fingers. The signal! Jane edged over to the left but Nancy frowned her back. Oh, of course. This curve was really going to fly over home plate. Nancy crooked her wrist and threw! The girl at the bat just dropped to the ground when she saw the ball coming and she let it go. And the ball really did come right over home plate only it was way up in the air, way, way up in the air and spinning swiftly toward the library window, for it did its veering later than calculated. Jane leapt in the air in an effort to catch it but she missed.

"Rufus! Rufus!" she yelled, and she closed her eyes and stuck her fingers in her ears, waiting for the crash.

Just in the nick of time Rufus jumped for the ball. He caught it in his left hand before it could crash through the window. He sprinted over with the ball.

"We'd better move the bases again," said Nancy. And they all moved farther away from the library.

"Stay here," said Jane to Rufus, pleadingly. So Rufus stayed and he said since he had caught the ball the girl was out, and why not have punch now? Jane gave him a nudge. This was real baseball and he mustn't think about anything

else. The girl said it didn't count that Rufus caught the ball, for he was the back-stop and not on the team. Even so, she graciously permitted Nancy's team a turn at the bat now, because the Busy Bees had had a long enough inning. They had run up such a big score she was sure the F. F. could never come up to it.

"That's the way with baseball," thought Jane. "Whoever is first at the bat usually wins."

Nancy was the first one up of the Fatal Four. The captain of the Busy Bee baseball team did not throw curves. Nancy struck at the first ball. It was a hit. She easily made first base. Now Jane was at the bat. Rufus, who decided to play back-stop for the foreign team as well as Jane's, was pounding his fist into his mitt to get some real atmosphere into this game.

While the pitcher was winding her arm around and around, Jane was busy too. She was swinging the bat, limbering up. At last, she thought. At last she was at the bat. That's all she liked to do in baseball. Bat! And so far she hadn't had a chance. And she swung herself completely around in her enthusiasm. Unfortunately the bat flew out of her hand and it hit Rufus on the forehead.

Rufus was staggered and saw stars. However, he tossed it off saying, "Aw, it didn't hurt," even though a lump began to show. Jane rubbed his forehead, and thereafter she swung with more restraint. Even so, the catcher and Rufus automatically stepped back a few paces whenever Jane was at

the bat, taking no chances with another wallop.

But now the pitcher pitched. Jane, still subdued and repressed, merely held the bat before her. Bang! The ball just came up and hit it and rolled halfway toward the pitcher. Both the pitcher and the catcher thought the other was going to run for the ball. Therefore neither one ran, and Jane made first base easily, putting Nancy on second. Now the bases were full because that's all the bases they had. And it was Clara Pringle at the bat.

The situation was too grave for Clara. She did not want to bat. How could she ever face Nancy if she struck out? Nancy and Jane might never speak to her again if she struck out. Besides, she had hurt her wrist pulling up a stubborn pie-weed when she was in outfield. She looked at Jane, who was dancing toward second, and Nancy, who was dancing toward home, impatiently waiting for the hit that would send them in. Clara gulped at her position of unexpected responsibility. When she joined the Fatal Four she had never envisioned being in a spot like this. She raised her hand to make a request.

"Can Rufus pinch hit for me because I hurt my wrist?" she asked timidly.

Rufus did not wait for anybody to say yes or no. He threw his mitt at Clara and seized the bat, pounding the

ground, the home plate, and an old bottle. That's the way he warmed up, and if Jane had been vociferous at the bat, Rufus was nothing short of a tornado.

"Stand still!" yelled the pitcher. "You make me dizzy."

Rufus swung at imaginary balls.

"Hey!" exclaimed the pitcher. "He's left-handed."

"Sure," said Jane. "Why not?"

"You call 'em southpaws," said Nancy. "I pitch good to him myself."

"Well, here goes," said the pitcher. "It just looks funny if you're not used to 'em." And she swung her arm around and around again.

While she was warming up and while Rufus was stomping around, swinging the bat, waiting for the ball, Spec Cullom, the ice-man, came along Elm Street. Evidently he saw in an instant that this was a real game and not just practice, for he stopped his team, threw down the iron weight to anchor his horse, Charlie, and strode into the lot and straddled the nearest log in the bleachers to watch. Rufus saw him and became even more animated with the bat.

At the same moment the twelve o'clock whistle blew. Now all the children were supposed to go home to lunch. The Busy Bees were in favor of stopping, but the Fatal Four protested. Here they were with all bases full and they should certainly play the inning out at least.

So the pitcher pitched and Rufus struck. Crack! He hit

the ball! Up and up it sailed, trailing the black tape it was wound with behind it like the tail of a kite!

As it disappeared from sight in the pine grove, Nancy ran to home plate and Jane ran to second base, and then home, and Rufus tore to first, and then to second and then home. And so it was a home run that had been hit.

"A home run!" everybody yelled in excitement. It was surprising that that hit had not broken a window, and the outfielder of the visiting team ran in search of the ball. But she couldn't find it and Clara joined her, for she was an experienced outfielder, but she couldn't find it either. Then the whole Busy Bee baseball team ran and looked for the ball, but they couldn't find it. So they all went home. The captain, impressed by the home run, yelled to Nancy that the score must have been a tie and they'd come back in a week or so to see who was the champ.

Jane and Nancy ran over to the pine grove to look for the ball. They hunted in the corner of the lot where skunk cabbage grew thick and melon vines covered a dump, covered even the sign that said DO NOT DUMP. They searched through the long field grass on this side of the library, trying not to get the thick bubbly-looking dew on their bare legs. Was this really snake spit as Joey and Rufus claimed, Jane wondered. If it was, where were all the snakes? She'd never seen a single snake. But where was the ball? That was some home run!

"You don't suppose he batted it clear across Elm Street into that lot, do you?" asked Nancy incredulously.

"Might have," said Jane, not knowing whether to be proud or ashamed. And the two girls crossed the street to take a look, just in case Rufus had swung as mighty an arm as that.

Rufus did not join in the search. He ran around from base to base to home plate, again and again, in ever widening circles until his course led him to the ice-man. The ice-man was one of his favorite people in Cranbury.

"Here," said Spec, "catch." And he threw the missing baseball to Rufus. "I yelled to the team that I caught the ball, but they couldn't hear me, I guess, what with whistles blowing and all the cheers. Some batter!" he said. "Keep it up, fella, and maybe next spring you can be bat boy for the South End baseball team."

The ice-man rolled a cigarette, using the last of the tobacco from his Bull Durham tobacco pouch, and he handed the empty bag to Rufus. "Here, fella," he said. "Put this in your pocket."

Rufus grinned, stuffed the pouch in his pocket, grabbed the ball, and tore off to the other end of the field where Nancy and Jane, wearied and hot, had given up looking for the ball. Then they all went home to lunch.

"Goodness!" said Mama, when she saw Rufus and Jane. "What have you been playing to get so banged up?"

"Just baseball," said Jane, drinking a long glass of water thirstily.

After lunch Rufus went back across the street and sat down to watch the men dig out the cellar. He thought about being bat boy for the South End baseball team and he pounded the old taped baseball into his fist, his left fist. And he thought about the Fatal Four. He was practically a member, and if the Fatal Four could not do without him for baseball, they'd naturally include him for punch and cookies if they ever reached that stage. He smiled to himself. The South End baseball team and the Fatal Four. That made two things he almost belonged to now.

5

TWO MOFFATS GO CALLING

JOEY HAD A CERTAIN WAY HE WALKED HOME FROM
school. He did not walk up one street and down the next,
turning sharp corners. He had it all figured out how he
could cut cater-corners across streets, how he could walk
from the south-east corner of this one to the north-west
corner of that one, and he knew that he saved at least one
whole block, if not more, by walking home from school

this way. Joey always walked: he never ran.

Jane always walked home from school with Nancy Stokes or she raced a trolley car. Rufus ran as fast as he could. He always was the first person out of the school yard, the first one up the street, and the first one home. That's because he was the hungriest boy in school and had to get home in a hurry. He could eat anything, though he preferred something like pie.

"You'll eat bread if you're so hungry," said Mama.

Sylvie didn't go to regular school any more. She went to Art School on the trolley. But she did run home from the trolley. Joey was the only one who didn't run, and that was because he had this special way of walking home and measuring his steps and cutting across lots and studying how to get home by the shortest possible route. He did not stop along the way.

"Hi, Joey!" somebody would yell.

"Hi!"

"Want to play ball?"

"Can't," he'd answer, not looking away from the point he was heading for. If he looked, he might be tempted to stop. He had no time for ball. And on he went.

On one block Joey stayed right on the sidewalk and did not cut cater-corners. There was a high board fence here and someone had drawn a lot of initials in white chalk. In one place there was a large chalk heart and inside of this there were the initials J.M. and M.J. with an arrow plunged recklessly through the whole.

J.M. could be Joey Moffat. M.J. could be Mary Jetting. He always wondered when he passed this fence who had drawn the heart with these initials in it. Mary Jetting was nobody he cared anything about, just a girl in some room or other at school. Room Nine, he thought. The chalk was beginning to wash off and the initials to grow faint. He never stopped to look at this heart on the fence, of course, but he liked to take a side-long glance at it as he walked past. He'd punch the fellow in the nose if he knew who put it there though.

He turned into Elm Street and, as he did so, a long red open touring car sailed by. "My car," thought Joey, and he remembered about Miss Myles, a teacher he had when he was in the first grade. This teacher still sent him letters and Christmas cards. He had not been the teacher's pet. Nobody was. But when he left Room One and went into

Room Two, he still remembered his old teacher. He had found a picture of a long red automobile with a lady wearing a veil riding in it. This lady was supposed to be Miss Myles. And he was supposed to be the one driving the car. He had made Mama write on it, "I will take you for a ride in this kind of an automobile some day," and send it to Miss Myles. Now she always wrote asking when she was going to have that ride.

Sometimes she sent him a limerick she had made up. Once she stuck a real dime and a real raisin on the limerick instead of using the words "dime" and "raisin." Rufus ate off the raisin before anyone could stop him but Joey had kept the dime for years, until one day, when Mama didn't have any money, he bought a loaf of bread with it. But you could still see the place on the paper where the dime had been stuck. He kept the limerick with his things. That was years ago and they still wrote cards and jokes. No more with dimes and raisins, though. That was just once. Mama made up Joey's jokes for him. But he drew plenty of pictures with long red automobiles that he was going to take Miss Myles riding in.

As Joey cut across a lot, not going by the winding path

that many feet had trodden down, but seeing a shorter, straighter, more direct route through the grass, he thought he should visit Miss Myles. He'd been thinking this for a long time. She was a good friend and he had never visited her. He came up the slope and onto the sidewalk and scraped the grass and loose dirt off his shoes. Yes, he should visit her. "Hello, Miss Myles." "Hello, Joe. Well, when are you going to take me for that ride?" "Oh, some day." The talk would go like that.

Joe turned into the long walk that led to the Moffats' house. Phew! The way the leaves were falling! And he just raked them up yesterday. You could rake these leaves up sixteen times a day and there'd still be leaves. Then he wondered if he had done right to cross Green Street from Mrs. Park's driveway over to Mrs. Lane's driveway. He calculated he might possibly have saved more steps had he walked from corner to corner. He'd try it that way tomorrow. It would be good if he had a pedometer.

He went up on the porch, stepped over Mr. Abbot's rubbers, and went into the house. He didn't go into the dining room where Mama or Sylvie was sewing on the machine, because he figured Mr. Abbot was in there too. Mr. Abbot was the man who had just gotten Joey the job of dusting the pews of the church and helping the sexton. Supposing Mr. Abbot asked him if he had dusted the pews yet for this week. He'd have to say no, not so far. He planned to do that tomorrow.

Nobody was in the kitchen. Joe was looking for Jane, but first he took a piece of bread and, since he had eaten his share of butter this noon, he spread it with apple butter. Butter was scarce and Mama had to divide it. Then he went out the back door looking for Jane. There were two things he wanted to ask her before he went for his papers. Rufus was bent over beside the back stoop, making something. He was working hard with his hammer and nailing some big crates together. And there was Jane! She was sitting on the back fence, waiting for Nancy Stokes probably. Joe put his hands on the top of the fence and swung himself up.

"H'lo," he said.

" 'Lo," said Jane.

They sat in silence for a while. One of the two things that Joe had in mind to ask her about was this: was M.J. in Jane's room in school? He thought she came from that end of the hall. Oh, well, what was the sense asking? What difference did it make anyway? The other matter was easier to approach. Miss Myles and her limericks to him and his red automobiles to her were old stories to all the Moffats. They were all very much interested in Miss Myles and how she always remembered Joey.

"I thought some day I'd go and visit Miss Myles," said Joe.

"Miss Myles!"

"Yeh," said Joe.

"Gee, yeh," said Jane. "I think you should. She likes you."

"Yeh."

"When are you goin'?"

"I dunno."

"Well, I mean are you goin' soon? Or are you goin' to wait until you're grown up and have that big red automobile?"

"Oh . . . soon."

"Uh-hum."

Then they just sat there again for a while without saying anything, thinking.

Finally Joey said, "Do you want to go with me?"

"Do you want me to?"

"Yeh, I don't want to go alone."

"Sure, I'll go," said Jane. Somehow she felt honored. Joe was asking her to go with him to see a special friend of his. Miss Myles was not a special friend of any of the rest of the Moffats. She was not like Mr. Abbot, the curate, who took them all, even Mama, to the circus. Jane thought Joe was awfully nice to ask her to come along. "When'll we go?" she asked.

Joe thought for some minutes.

"How about tonight?" he said.

"After supper?"

"Yeh."

"Gee," said Jane. "That's a real visit, isn't it? Going after supper like that. It's a real call, that's what it is."

"Yeh," said Joe. "I thought we might go after supper." And he jumped down and went off to get his newspapers. It was time to deliver them.

So after supper they both washed their hands and faces and Joe wet his hair down so that it wouldn't stand up straight in the middle of his head like telegraph poles. Joe put on a clean blouse and Jane a clean dress, not her best dress but just a clean one. Then they told Mama where they were going. She seemed very pleased. She said to give her regards to Miss Myles and kissed them good-by.

Rufus had been watching these preparations. "Can I go too?" he asked. "I could wear my gloves."

Rufus was the only one of the four Moffats who had gloves to wear even when it was warm. He wore Hughie Pudge's old ones. They were all kid gloves and they just fitted him. The other Moffats wore mittens in the winter but they never wore anything on their hands at all unless it was cold. But Rufus had lots of these gloves that he could wear winter or summer. He rarely remembered about them but the preparations that Joe and Jane were making convinced him that tonight was the night for his kid gloves.

He followed Joe and Jane to the door. "Can I go too?" he repeated, waving his kid gloves at them.

"No, fella," said Joe. "You can blow up my football."

"Right," said Rufus. He was happy to blow up Joe's football. He was not often permitted to do this.

Joe and Jane went out. It was a soft misty night in October. They looked back at the house. Mama had put the little lamp in the small square stained-glass window over the porch. The light shone gold and red through the mist and cast a warm glow. They turned down the street towards Elm Street.

"I hope we'll know what to talk about," said Jane. "When you pay a visit you have to talk."

"Yeh, I was thinkin' so too," said Joe.

Joe certainly had been thinking about the conversation and planning what to talk about. There was plenty to talk about if he could say it. He wasn't good at talking, not to grown-ups.

"You should do most of the talkin'," said Jane, "because you're the one she likes. She doesn't even know me. I didn't even have her in Room One."

"Yeh . . ." said Joe.

"If you get stuck, I'll put in a word now and then if I can think of anything."

"Uh-huh," said Joe. And he fell silent, thinking about what he'd say. So far he could think of four things to say. First he would tell Miss Myles about a certain plan he had for raising silver foxes. He had read an ad. in the *Popular Mechanics* at the library and it was as easy as pie. Anybody could get rich off of silver foxes. When all the Moffats were rich off this business, he'd drive around some day, pick Miss Myles up in that long red automobile they talked about, and take her for a ride along the shore.

The silver foxes and the red automobile made two things to talk about. Also he planned to tell her he still had all the cards she'd ever sent and that you could still see where the dime and the raisin had been stuck. And finally he could say that Mama sent her regards. Or he could say that first.

Anyway, first or last, it made four things. He began to whistle.

Joe and Jane walked the longest way from their house on Ashbellows Place to Miss Myles' house on Thomas Street over near the railroad tracks. They crunched on some apples from Mrs. Stokes' apple orchard. Joe had another in his pocket for Miss Myles. If you counted the apple, he had five things to talk about.

They did not take any short cuts and they didn't race. They walked over there and all the way Joe thought about the things he'd say. They stopped for a moment on the corner of Miss Myles' street to watch an express train go streaking past. The people inside the train looked warm and comfortable, reading their papers or looking out the windows. Joey and Jane waved and then they slowly continued to Miss Myles' house.

"This is it. This is number seventeen," Joe whispered.

"Yeh," said Jane. And then, to bolster their morale, she added, "You know, this is really an awfully nice thing to do —coming to see her like this. She's gonna be awfully pleased to see you."

"Hm-m-m," said Joe.

They stood quietly on the sidewalk, looking at the house.

"There's a light in there," said Jane.

"Means she's home," said Joey.

They looked at the house. It was a small inviting house. There wasn't too long a veranda to tiptoe across. Just a couple of steps up, a little porch to cross, and they'd be at the door. They finished their apples and threw the cores across the street. Then Joe started slowly up the street.

"Let's walk around the block," he suggested.

"Yeh," said Jane.

So they walked around the block and Joey slowly revolved in his mind all the points of conversation. Silver foxes, long red touring car, the cards, the regards, and the apple. These would certainly take a long time to tell and when they were told they could go home.

And here they were back in front of Miss Myles' house. This time Joey surprised Jane by walking right up on the porch. She had thought they probably would walk around the block at least once or twice more, maybe the whole evening, and then go home.

Joey held his finger over the bell. Five things to talk about, counting the apple. He pressed the bell in. It rang with a startling suddenness, making Joey and Jane jump. And almost instantaneously they found themselves bathed in light as someone inside switched on the porch bulb. They blinked their eyes and wiped their hands on their coats, hoping they were still clean.

A lady opened the door.

"Who is it?" she asked.

Miss Myles and Joey had not seen each other for a long time. They only just wrote to each other. Joey scarcely recognized her. And Miss Myles didn't recognize him either.

"Yes?" she said kindly.

"She thinks we're selling something or that we want her to join the Red Cross," thought Jane. Joe didn't say anything. Nobody said anything. Jane was just about to say, "This is Joey," when to her relief Miss Myles said:

"Why, Joey Moffat, come in! Come right in. And I suppose this is Jane. And where's my red automobile, young man?"

Joe smiled but said nothing. They all went in and sat down on Miss Myles' wicker furniture.

"So you came to take me for a ride in that red automobile

of yours?" Miss Myles said again.

Joey smiled and stared at the ceiling. But he didn't say anything. Then he looked at a porcelain cat that was supposed to keep the door from swinging and he kept looking at this cat for the rest of the evening. It was not easy to talk about the red automobile. And if he did talk about it, how could he jump from that to silver foxes? That's what Joe wondered, and it kept him from saying anything about red automobiles or silver foxes either. Nobody said anything for a while. Everybody's wicker chairs creaked. Jane thought now was the time when she should put in a word. She was uncomfortable too, though not as uncomfortable as Joe because, after all, Miss Myles was his particular friend and she scarcely knew Jane. She only knew about her. Joey sometimes mentioned her and the other Moffats in his cards to Miss Myles.

"Yes," repeated Miss Myles. "When I saw you at the door, Joey, I thought, ah, now here's where I get a ride in a beautiful red automobile."

Joe smiled on one side of his mouth. He shouldn't sit here grinning like that Cheshire cat. He knew that. He rehearsed in his mind. "I saw an ad. Just an ad. about silver foxes . . ." Jane thought of something to say. She thought she could say Joe was going to save up for a red automobile. But she didn't say it because so far Joey hadn't said anything and he was the one should do the talking. At least he should talk first.

Joe thought, well, now they had talked about the red automobile, at least Miss Myles had, and if he could think how to begin he'd discuss this plan he had of raising silver foxes. It didn't sound good to him to start with, "I saw an ad." He was just going to plunge in when his chair creaked loud. Very loud. The chair creaking like this made him realize how he'd sound when he began to talk. There was silence now. Then he'd talk. How'd his voice sound? Like that creak? He couldn't be sure how his voice would turn out. Sometimes it came out loud. Sometimes it came out in a high squeak. How could he count on it sounding like any ordinary voice? He had forgotten about his voice when he came here. He brushed his hand over his hair. Some of it was rearing up like telegraph poles again.

Jane thought the conversation was not going very well. In conversation one person was supposed to say something. Then another person. Then the first. Then another. No long silences in between times, especially when you pay a call. Silences are all right when you make a long visit, say for several days, because no one could keep up a conversation all that time. But in a short visit like this she and Joe and Miss Myles ought to talk and they weren't.

Miss Myles said something now and then but neither Joey nor Jane answered, because they both were so busy thinking they should talk and embarrassed because they weren't.

How long was everybody going to sit here like this, Jane wondered, squirming her toes around inside her shoes. By rights she shouldn't do the talking. Joey should, because this lady was his friend. But Jane finally realized that Joey had reached such a state of shyness he was not going to be able to say one thing. She felt desperate. "I'll have to talk," she thought. And maybe, if she kept the conversation strictly on Joe, she would not be stealing his show.

"Joey has the best memory of all of us," she ventured bravely.

"I'm sure he has," agreed Miss Myles, "because he always remembers that he promised me a ride in a long red automobile."

"He remembers all dates," said Jane.

"My!"

"I don't mean just dates like when Columbus discovered America and Washington's birthday. I mean *all* dates."

"Goodness!"

"He remembers things like what date the parish house burned down and the New Haven depot too. And the day Rufus fell out of the cherry tree, and the day Rufus got his bike."

"Gracious!"

"Yes. He remembers what date the parish house burned down," Jane repeated. "Don't you, Joe?" She looked at him encouragingly.

Joe nodded. Jane had hoped he'd answer the right date. But he didn't, he just nodded.

"Sure. And he remembers when the New Haven depot burned down. Don't you, Joe?"

Joe nodded again.

"Nodding isn't exactly conversation but it is taking part," thought Jane. Out loud, she said, "He doesn't have to write them down."

To this Miss Myles just raised her eyebrows incredu-

busly.

"The funny thing is that most of these things happened in May and still Joey remembers them."

"In May?"

"Yes. The month of May."

Here Jane paused and she looked desperately at Joe. He could slide in now if he felt like it. He didn't feel like it, though. His forehead was damp. Jane plunged on.

"Yes. So many things happened in May, like birthdays in our family, but he keeps them all straight and doesn't mix them up with the fires."

Miss Myles had settled herself comfortably in her arm chair and she nodded her head up and down, up and down, considering this. But she didn't say anything, so Jane continued.

"If you say to Joe, 'Joe, when did the parish house burn down?' he doesn't have to think a second. He says right off, 'May third.'"

"May third!"

"I don't mean the parish house really burned down on May third. He knows the date. I don't."

Jane saw that Miss Myles looked a little confused.

"I'm just saying May third because I don't know the date and I'm just saying May third." This was hard to explain and the perspiration broke out on Jane's forehead now.

"I might have said the fifth!" she blurted out. "That's because I don't know the date. Only Joey knows in our whole family."

Miss Myles touched her handkerchief to her nose. Was everything clear? Jane wondered.

"I just said May third because it came into my head first."

"Well," said Miss Myles, turning to Joe with a slightly bewildered air, "the parish house did or did not burn down on May third?"

This required an answer. Joe said, "May eighteenth!"

And "May eighteenth" were the only two words that Joe said during the whole visit. Then Miss Myles left the room for a moment. Joe and Jane moved to the door. When Miss Myles came back, she gave each one of them a big round lemon cookie with a scalloped edge and they left.

The air smelled sweet, of ripe apples and grapes. They walked home, not saying anything until they were around the corner. They passed warmly lighted houses and in some you could see the men smoking their pipes and reading the paper. And in another someone was playing the piano. In another a lot of ladies laughed. Joey whistled softly. When the children reached their corner, they went around to the back yard, climbed up on the fence, reached for some bunches of ripe purple grapes, and started eating them and spitting out the skins.

"Taste better at night than in the day, don't they?" said Jane.

"Yeh. Dew on 'em," said Joe.

"I wouldn't 'ave talked because she's really your friend, and I shouldn't 'ave done all the talkin'," said Jane apologetically. She did not want Joe to think she had deliberately stolen his show.

"Yeh," said Joe. "I should 'a' talked."

"Gee, it's hard to talk sometimes, isn't it?" said Jane.

"Yeh, it sure is hard to talk," said Joey. "I had a lot to tell her when I went in there," he went on, "but when I got in there I couldn't talk."

"I have a hard time talkin' too," said Jane. "But sometimes I can make myself."

"Yeh? Well, I couldn't tonight. Talkin' sure is hard."

Rufus came out of the back door, leaving it open so that a path of light stretched into the yard.

"I heard you come home," he said. He shinnied up on the back fence and sat in the light from the kitchen. Joey reached up and felt around for a big bunch of grapes for him. And Joey also gave Rufus the apple they had meant for Miss Myles. He wondered how they had forgotten to give it to her.

"Go to Miss Myles'?" asked Rufus.

"Uh-huh."

"The lady in the red automobile?"

"Yeh."

"Rufe," said Jane, "can you talk?"

"Sure," said Rufus. "I got a tongue, ain't I?" And he stuck out his tongue and wagged it at them.

6

EYES IN THE PIPES

"SOMETHING MUST BE DONE ABOUT THE SEWERS," SAID the Town Improvement Association. "And something must be done about the drains at the street corners so we do not have all this mud!" they cried, and they did not stop campaigning until the town finally decreed that new sewers must be dug and that new drains must be made. Therefore one day men with pickaxes and shovels moved up and down the streets, digging deep trench-like ditches and lining the sides of the streets with big, round, dark red clay pipes.

Rufus was happy when at last the workers reached Pleasant Street and Ashbellows Place. The air smelled of gas fumes all the time and of damp red dirt. Since Rufus was the first one home from school, he was the first to see that the sewers had reached their street.

"A tunnel!" he shouted, and he stooped over and entered the first red pipe, crawling through it and then the next and the next, all the way down the street. Sometimes the pipes fitted together neatly and there would be two or even three pipes to crawl through without seeing the sky.

When the other children in the neighborhood came home from school, they were delighted too. No longer need they go over to Clark Street for crawling through the pipes. Here were their own, right here! Everybody wore tremendous holes in the knees of his stockings as the game of stump-the-leader took on new life.

"Follow me!" yelled Rufus, balancing precariously on the shiny rounded surface of one of the pipes and leaping down to crawl through the next.

Moreover there were ditches in the middle of the road to race through when the men had finished their work and gone away. Before they left they always placed smoky red lanterns and tar torches every few feet along the high piles of freshly turned dirt. Of course there was a watchman to keep things in order while the workers were gone, but he stayed in, or near, a little wooden tool shed at the corner of Elm Street. Red and green lanterns hung from the door of it. There were a great many colored lights now, including the regular purple carbon street lamps along Elm Street and it was a pretty sight to see them all flickering on a dark night.

"Like Christmas," said Rufus.

People had to stay on the side of the street they found themselves on. For instance, if you were on the Moffats' side of the street and wished you were on Mr. Buckle's, the oldest inhabitant's, side, you had to go all the way to Elm Street or Rock Avenue to cross over; that is, if you were a grown-up. Children, of course, had no difficulty scrambling up the hill and down into the ditch and up the other side. But grown-ups had to stay on the side of the street they were on.

Jane liked this commotion as much as Rufus. "Hello!" she yelled at the oldest inhabitant. "Hello!" he yelled back, putting his hands to his mouth and making a funnel with them, as though he were miles away at sea.

These pipes and ditches stayed in a state of semi-completion for a long time on the Moffats' street. The trenches were dug, the pipes were ready to be installed, but there they stayed. The men who were working on them had not come for some weeks.

"They forgot this block," said Rufus happily, for the sewers had been finished on every other street in town. All the streets had a gentle swell along the middle where the new sewers had been dug. But on the Moffats' street the pipes were still there to crawl through, the dirt hills made good slides to belly-flop down when the snow and ice came, and the ditches were excellent for war games.

Every day, when Rufus ran home from school, he stooped down at the corner of Pleasant Street and crawled through the pipes to Ashbellows Place until he reached his house. One day he bent over and entered the first pipe as usual and started to crawl through. In the distance ahead of him, however, he saw two eyes shining in the dark, two green eyes. Rufus hastily backed out. Somebody was in there! Rufus climbed on top of the first pipe, lay on his stomach, hung his head over the edge, and looked in. The eyes were still shining green and they had not come any nearer.

"Hey!" said Rufus.

The eyes just stared.

"Who are you?" said Rufus.

The eyes did not blink.

"Come out," said Rufus.

The eyes shone green.

"You're nobody," said Rufus.

The eyes flickered. They seemed to come a little nearer and to turn yellow.

"Criminenty!" thought Rufus. "This isn't a person. This is an animal. Maybe it's a wild animal—a wolf or a fox maybe."

Of course there were no wolves or foxes in Cranbury, but neither were there any alligators and yet somebody had once caught a small alligator in the marshes at the shore near Orchard Grove. Nobody knew where it came from. It was a great mystery and people were still speculating. Since an alligator had been found in Cranbury, it was not too incredible to find a wolf or a fox occasionally. At least that is what Rufus thought as he stared in the pipes at these gleaming eyes.

No, you couldn't be absolutely certain that these eyes did not belong to a wolf or a fox. While Rufus was convincing himself of this, the eyes disappeared like lights going out. Whatever it was must have turned around and gone the other way.

Naturally Rufus did not crawl in after it. Rufus was cautious. He raced as fast as he could to the corner of Elm Street and he looked in at that end of the pipes. There they were! The eyes in the pipes! Gleaming yellow eyes!

"There you are!" said Rufus in excitement. He pursed up his lips. "Come on, come on," he coaxed, the way one does dogs or cats.

The longer Rufus looked at those eyes the more certain he became that they belonged to a wolf. "Come here, wolf," he said. He was not scared because he was very near his own home and after all the wolf was in the pipes. However, he was not going to run around crying, "Wolf! Wolf!" the way the boy did in the story of "The Sheep and the Wolf." He had come across that story in every schoolroom he had been in so far, Room One, Room Two, and Room Three. Also it was in a big book of stories the Moffats owned, and sometimes Jane or Joe read it out loud at home. He knew what the story meant very well, and he knew better than to run off and yell, "Wolf! Wolf!" arousing everybody in the town, until he had proof these eyes in these pipes were wolf eyes. Otherwise nobody would ever believe him if he really did see a wolf. You have to be careful, he cautioned himself. Of course, if Joey or Jane came along he could tell them. But not the town.

But if this animal never came out of the pipe, how could anyone tell what it was? He might not come out. He might stay in there. It was a nice safe place to be. What'd he do though when the men came back and started putting these pipes down in the ditch where they belonged? Then he'd have to come out and roam.

It is not good to have a wolf roaming around town. Or any other animal, a lion, a tiger, or a fox. Rufus decided to catch him. He would get a lasso and wait on top of this pipe and catch him when he tried to get out.

Suppose the animal went out the other end of the pipes while he was watching this! He ought to find someone to guard that end. Right now the eyes were still watching him. They stared at Rufus unblinkingly. Rufus couldn't look so long without winking. He had to wink often.

"Stay there," said Rufus. Nobody was around to guard either end, so Rufus ran home as fast as he could, around to the back yard and into the entry where he found a piece of clothesline for a lasso. Jane was not at home. She was out with Nancy Stokes trying to get Red Cross members, Mama said. And Joey, of course, was still delivering his papers.

Rufus took a piece of bread and dashed out the front door, stepping over Mr. Abbot's rubbers. Mr. Abbot must have been in the dining room, trying on cassocks. There wasn't any sense asking him to help, because a grown-up probably would not have the patience to stalk the animal. Rufus went back to the corner and looked in the pipes. The eyes were gone. He ran down to the other end of the pipe line and looked in. Still no eyes! Maybe the animal had gone to sleep. He certainly had not come out in this little while when Rufus had been gone, not in broad daylight anyway, not if he were a wild animal anyway, Rufus reasoned.

"Where are you, wolf?" he asked. He wanted to get in

the pipes and crawl through now. But, of course, with this animal in there that was impossible. He hoped he'd see the animal again. Otherwise how would anybody have the nerve to crawl through the pipes again? They'd always think, "Is the animal in there or isn't it?"

Rufus lay on his stomach on top of the pipe and he kept his eyes glued to the darkness inside. He did not see the eyes. Hughie Pudge came along and asked him what he was doing. Rufus told him to go down to the other corner and see if he could see anything in the pipes. Hughie did so but he soon tired of looking at nothing and said he had to go home. So Rufus went home too.

He sat down on the porch. Catherine-the-cat was sitting in the last pale glow of the sun. Catherine was beginning to look old and worn. One side of her gray coat was singed a light brown because she always sat in the same position on the little swinging door over the grate of the kitchen stove.

"You should turn around and bake the other side once in a while," said Rufus. But Catherine-the-cat just closed her eyes in complete boredom.

Jane came running around from the back yard. "It's a long, long way to Tipperary," she was singing. She felt good because three ladies had joined the Red Cross and that made seven members she had gotten so far, if you could count Mrs. Price who kept saying she was going to join but didn't have any change today.

"Hey, Jane," Rufus yelled above her singing. "There's an animal—a fox, a lion, or something, with green eyes in the pipes. I seen him from both ends. Sometimes the eyes look yellow."

"Uh-hum," said Jane. "Where'd it come from?" She really thought this was one of Rufus's jokes.

Rufus could tell she thought he was joking. He was disgusted. "How do I know where it *came* from! All I know is its eyes gleam."

The way he said "gleam" sent shivers up and down Janey's spine. Maybe he wasn't joking. Sometimes animals escaped from somewhere.

"Goodness!" said Jane. "What's it gonna do? Is it gonna stay in there? When's it gonna go away? It oughtta be caught. It'll get up there in the woods by the reservoir and then who'll want to go up there and have picnics and pick violets?"

"Well, it's not in the woods now. It's in the pipes, rest-ing," said Rufus. "So long as *it* is in the pipes though, *we* can't go in the pipes."

"Aw," said Jane, not believing again. "Can't be a *wild* animal. Not in Cranbury."

Now Rufus became really irritated. "Jane," he said in exasperation, "don't say *can't*. You never can be sure. One animal might have gotten away from somewhere."

Again Jane felt the shivers up and down her spine. Except for that alligator there never had been a wild animal in Cranbury. But there might be one. Rufus could tell she was more sympathetic in her attitude.

"Want to see if we can see him now?" he invited her.

Jane hugged her knees. "Supposin' he comes out while we're lookin'?"

"He'll be just as scared of us as us of him," said Rufus. "If he was in the woods, he probably wouldn't be as scared. Here in front of our own house we're the ones shouldn't be as scared. Besides, I'm gonna lasso him."

They went down the walk with Catherine-the-cat blinking her eyes in the sun and looking after them disdainfully. They met Joey coming up the street, balancing himself on the pipes.

"Hey, Joey," said Rufus. " 'S'an animal in the pipes. A wolf or something. A fox, maybe."

Joey stopped, interested. Rufus wasn't joking. He was talking as though he meant it. Joe was a sensible fellow and it did not seem at all preposterous to him that there might be a fox in the pipes. Especially a silver fox! Take this, for instance. Say somebody else in Cranbury had been reading the same ads. he had been reading in the *Popular Mechanics* about raising silver foxes, and say this person had gone ahead and found the money to buy some, might not one easily have escaped? Of course! What luck, thought Joe. If he could catch this silver fox, and if the owner never claimed him, why, that was the beginning of his silver fox business!

The three children took turns peering in. Darkness was all they saw. Where were the eyes? After a long time, Rufus thought he saw them. It was like staring down the railroad tracks in the night-time, waiting for the express to come, and seeing and not seeing and finally being sure you saw the headlight miles and miles down the track. Now he thought he saw the eyes. Then he didn't. Then he really did see them.

"Look!" he whispered to Joe.

Joey looked.

"You're right, fella," he said excitedly. "There he is, all right!"

Jane shivered. She took one quick look. She saw the gleaming eyes and she hopped onto the next pipe. "Goodness!" she said.

To Joey these eyes looked like fox eyes. He was sure of it. And through his mind raced a vision of not one fox but a dozen or more. A whole silver fox business in fact, that could make the Moffats, well, not rich but . . .

The eyes came nearer. "Let me have your lasso, fella," said Joe. Rufus gave him his rope. But now the eyes stayed where they were. They came no nearer.

"Let's go and meet him," said Joe. "Naturally he's not just going to come out here and get himself caught."

"Inside?" asked Rufus, ready to crawl in.

"No. A cornered animal will strike," said Joe. "There are small openings all along the way between the pipes. He could get out of one of them and escape."

So they proceeded up the street, cautiously examining each opening. There were no eyes anywhere.

"They're out," said Rufus. He and Joey and Jane had reached the other end of the pipe line and they had not seen the eyes again. Disappointed, they went home to dinner.

That night after dinner Joey was reading the newspaper. Why, right on the front page, besides the war news, there were all kinds of stories about animals. A lady in Texas had a panther for a pet, a baby panther, and she wore it around her neck. In London a tiger had escaped from the zoo. Nearer home a deer had been seen in the woods on the Sleeping Giant. With animals anything was possible. Here were three different animals in three different spots in the world where you would hardly expect to find them. Maybe tomorrow there would be still another animal story in the paper. This story would tell how Rufus and Joey Moffat caught a fox, a silver fox, found wandering through the new sewer pipes in Cranbury.

All the Moffats were sitting or working around the kitchen range except Jane, who had run over to Nancy Stokes' house to learn "In Flanders Field" for school. They were going to learn the whole thing, every word, by heart. The thought of the fox or the wolf or whatever it was out there in the sewer pipes lent wings of fear to Janey's feet, and she practically flew over the fence from the Moffats' house to Nancy's.

Rufus was sitting in Mama's wicker sewing rocker right in front of the stove, reading. Rufus could read very well now. In fact he could read as fast as any of the Moffats. Last week he had read a whole book in one hour. It was fine print too. "Sink or Swim" was the name of it.

Sylvie was painting postcards at the kitchen table. She spent her free evenings painting Christmas, Easter, and birthday cards, and also everyday cards with pictures of sunsets and of ladies with wide hair ribbons around their heads. She took orders for these cards and received fifty cents a dozen or five cents apiece for them. The mail going out of Cranbury was full of sunsets and ladies now.

Mama was pressing the seams of a dress. S-s-s-s, hissed the steam as her hot iron came down on the damp cloth. The smell of the dye of the material filled the kitchen.

Joey turned the pages of the newspaper to the lost and found column. No fox was listed among the lost. Mostly dogs were lost. He was glad that no fox was mentioned. If someone had advertised for the fox, then of course the Moffats would have to give it right back to that person. But if no one advertised, the fox was his!

The first thing to do was to build the fox pen. If he had one fox, Joey was certain it would be very easy to add others, and soon he would have several. No! He laughed to himself. The first thing that he had to do was to catch that fox. "I'm actin' as though I already had that fox." Joey couldn't help grinning. "We just got to catch that fox out there," he thought, running his hand through the hair that stood up like telegraph poles on the top of his head. "Supposin' he gets away!"

But right now he felt as though a toothache were beginning. He went into the pantry to get a clove to put in his mouth. Just so it wouldn't get as bad as it was last night, that's all he hoped.

"Mr-r-r-r."

"Somebody let the cat out," said Mama.

Joey opened the door and out leaped Catherine-the-cat, disappearing into the night. Joey came back and stood over the stove, warming a piece of old red flannel and holding it against his cheek. After a while his toothache began to feel better. The flannel and the clove had helped.

Joey didn't say he had a toothache but everybody knew

he had one. Mama and Sylvie studied plans in their minds about how they could get Joey's teeth tended to. The heat from the flannel and the clove really did help Joey right now though, and he let his thoughts and dreams wander back to the silver fox.

"Hey, Rufe," he said.

"What," said Rufus, without looking up.

"Want to take a walk?"

"Don't go gallivanting around town at this time of the night," said Mama. "Rufus ought to be in bed anyway."

"We won't be gone a minute," Joey promised.

Rufus said, "Wait till I finish this chapter." But Joey gave him an urgent tug on his shoulder. "What's up?" thought Rufus. He looked at the page he was on, page seventy-three, and he closed the book. Rufus did not use book marks. He remembered the number of the page. He did not remember dates of fires and birthdays as Joey did, but he did remember the page he was on in a book. The two boys went out the back door.

"Thought I'd take a look at that fox out there," said Joe casually.

"Right," said Rufus. "Get my lasso."

Rufus found the rope and he and Joey went around the house to the street. The red lanterns and the gold flares of the flickering tar torches lighted the streets and looked like a mosaic.

"This time are we goin' in after him?" asked Rufus bravely.

"Naw . . . see if we can coax him out. He'll be hungry by now. I brought this piece of salt pork. Hope foxes like it. Hungry and frightened, that's what he'll probably be. He must be frightened or he'd have come out and tried to get back to the woods before this."

"Sure." But then Rufus added as an afterthought, "How do you know he didn't come out while we were having supper?"

"Well . . . if he's a woods fox, he might have come out and run off to the woods, and that'd be all right. But," and Joey's voice trembled slightly with excitement, "he *may* be an escaped silver fox, the kind they raise for fur. If that's what he is, then naturally he's frightened and I don't think he'd have come out."

"Good you thought of the bait," said Rufus. Any kind of animal would suit him. All he wanted was to be sure and catch the animal so that crawling through the pipes would be safe again.

Now they had reached the corner. The watchman was dozing in front of a fire he had built in an old ash can. His chair was tilted against the shed and his cap was pulled down over his eyes. Joey and Rufus stepped quietly in order not to waken him. They stooped over and looked in the pipe. They saw darkness, nothing but darkness.

"Wish we had a flashlight," said Rufus.

"We'll borrow one of these lanterns for a second," said Joe. He climbed up on the dirt and picked up a red lantern. He held it close within the opening. The lantern cast a red, mysterious glow. "Some tunnel!" muttered Rufus, and he wondered how he ever had had the courage to crawl through, wolf or no wolf, fox or no fox.

But right now, anyway, they didn't see a fox or a wolf, either awake or asleep. So Joey replaced the lantern and they ran down to the other corner. "Seems like he must still be in there," said Joe, beginning to doubt. All the same, they looked in hopefully, and in Joey's case at least, prayerfully.

"There they are!" yelled Rufus excitedly.

Sure enough! There were the eyes, shining golden in the

dark.

"Thank goodness!" murmured Joey in relief. A silver fox, a silver fox farm, he thought.

"But be quiet," he cautioned Rufus. "He's scared already. We don't want to scare him more. I'll put the bait here at the entrance. And I'll get on top of the pipe and when he comes out to eat, I'll grab him around the neck, hold on to his jugular vein the way they do in Jack London, and you can slip the rope around him so he can't get away. Then we'll walk him home."

This plan sounded simple, as though it were bound to work. Rufus squatted down about a foot in front of the pipe and watched the eyes.

"They're comin' nearer," he said.

"Sh-sh-sh, don't talk."

"He smells the bait," thought Joey.

"He can't see my eyes," thought Rufus. "You can only see animals' eyes. Not mine. A 'uman's don't shine in the dark." Rufus found comfort in this thought.

"The eyes are comin' nearer." Joe whispered it this time.

"He can't see us," whispered Rufus.

"Can smell us though," muttered Joe.

"If he's hungry he'll come out," said Rufus reassuringly, "whether he smells us or not."

Joe watched the eyes. Weren't they coming now? Just a little bit nearer? Yes, they were! Joey imagined putting his fingers into that soft fur and holding the silver fox so tight he couldn't get away. The beginning of his fox ranch! "Oh, knock wood," he prayed, feeling around in the dark for a plank, "that the real owner won't be found and that I can keep him!"

Now the eyes were really coming closer. The night was pitch black, with no moon and no stars. Only the feeble glow of the lanterns and torches. Up the street a way the purple carbon lamp cast an eerie circle of light. But Joey and Rufus were concentrating on these two phosphorescent eyes and felt they were the only lights in the world. They strained their own eyes, trying to see the kind of animal these eyes belonged to. In Joey's mind there was little doubt. A fox, a silver fox . . .

However, in Rufus's mind there were still many possibilities. A lion, a tiger, or a wolf. He thought of the picture of the sheep huddled together in a blizzard on the Moffats' sitting-room wall. They were huddled together not only to keep warm but because they feared wolves. Rufus looked away from the gleaming eyes for a moment and at the swaying lavender street lamp, and he saw moths and insects darting madly at it. A bat swooped swiftly by. All of a sudden Rufus felt scared. If this was a wolf in there, then what in the world was he doing here? That's what he wanted to know. Joey's talk of jugular veins was all right. But it was usually the wolf that did the springing for the jugular vein in real life; or at least in books.

He got up and climbed on the pipe behind Joe. "Hey, I can't catch him with you up here," said Joey.

"Let's go home," said Rufus.

"Not scared, are you, fella?" said Joe. "I'm ready for him. I'll catch him."

Joe bent over and looked in closely. The eyes were very near now, looking strangely wild and yellow. "Fox, all right," thought Joe. Inch by inch the eyes drew nearer! Salt pork was just the thing, thought Joe. All animals like salt. And where'd they find a salt lick in Cranbury? Nowhere. That's where this salt pork came in handy.

Joey seemed so sure this was a fox, and a fox was not as scary as a wolf, thought Rufus. A fox in the night-time was scary but not *as* scary. And murmuring, "I'm not scared," he resumed his position, lasso in hand. Phew! Those eyes were close!

"Still can't see him," said Joe.

"Let's get a torch again," suggested Rufus.

"No . . . scare him away again."

They waited. They waited for what seemed the whole night. Nobody came along the street fortunately, for they might have ruined the whole business.

All of a sudden the eyes came forward with a rush. Joey scrunched up his eyes, put his hands down, and caught hold of the animal right around its neck exactly as he had planned. His heart sank. *This fur did not feel like fox fur. It was short!* And the animal was too small to be anything but an ordinary . . .

Rufus slipped the lasso around it. "All right," said Joey. "Never mind the rope. Look what we caught." And he moved over to a lantern.

"Criminenty! Catherine-the-cat!" bellowed Rufus.

"Yeh, Catherine!" said Joey. And Catherine-the-cat it was, squirming and writhing and tying herself up in a ball. Joey set her down and she ran in the direction of home as fast as she could go.

"Criminenty!" said Rufus again.

But Joey began to laugh. "Some fox!" he said, and he laughed and laughed. Then he grew sober when he thought how he had figured on the animal being a silver fox.

Rufus began to laugh too. And he didn't stop when Joey did. He kept laughing and he wished Joey would laugh some more too. He laughed and laughed all the way home, louder and louder, hoping to make Joey laugh again.

But Joey didn't laugh any more. "Some fox!" he told himself.

7

MONEY IN THE ICE

"SETTLEMENT HOUSE!" SAID RUFUS IN DISGUST. "WHY DO they call it a *settlement* house?" He had come to the city cheerfully with Mama and Jane and Joey to watch Sylvie give a performance of "The Lollipop Princess," in the Settlement House for the benefit of the soldiers and sailors, even though he had already seen her in it at the Town Hall. He came because he expected to see Indians in a place with a name like that.

"Settlement House!" Rufus repeated. "I didn't see any Indians."

He was very disappointed. He had waited impatiently for today. Now, he had thought, he would see the kind of house the settlers lived in, made of logs, where people who looked like Daniel Boone lived, and where there would be plenty of Indians about; friendly ones on the inside, and hostile ones on the outside. But these people were not Indians or pioneers either.

And the settlement house itself looked just like any other ordinary red brick house from the outside. Inside there were just rooms. There was one big room with a stage in it. That's where the play was given. Also there was a kitchen where the people that ran the house cooked cocoa and piled cookies on paper plates. For a minute, when Rufus saw cocoa and cookies, he thought perhaps now the Indians or at least the pioneers would come. There was an upstairs to the house and maybe that was where they stayed. But everybody, all the ordinary people, drank their cocoa and no settlers joined in. Nor was there a trace of an Indian! Not so much as a feather or a tomahawk!

"Why didn't you tell me this was just a house?" he asked a little crossly. He and Mama, Jane, and Joey were picking their way up the street on the way to the trolley car. They were all walking gingerly on the ash-strewn pavements trying not to get cinders in their rubbers or to slip on a smooth spot. Sylvie had stayed behind in the Settlement House because she was giving "The Lollipop Princess" again tonight.

"Once I thought it meant Indians too," said Jane dreamily. "Stockades . . . blockades. But it doesn't."

Joey was silent. An uncomfortable thought had just struck him. The late afternoon was icy cold and the temperature might easily have fallen down around zero. And he or Mama or somebody should have remembered to turn off the water in the cellar before they left. Otherwise the pipes might have frozen. And if they had frozen they might have burst! For a while he kept this possibility to himself.

"It's called a Settlement House," said Mama, "because the people who manage it try to settle newcomers to the country and tell them the ways of the land."

"Any newcomer is really a sort of a settler," added Jane.

"Not if there aren't any Indians," said Rufus, still cross,

and having to run to keep up with the rest of the family.

Joey took Rufus by the hand. "Well, fella," he said, to take Rufus's mind off the dismal disappointment he had had of not seeing any Indians, "well, you better stop thinking about Indians and think instead of whether the pipes busted or not!"

"Gracious!" exclaimed Mama. "Did we forget to turn off the water? How could we have, on a day like this?"

"'Cause it's day-time," said Jane. This was true. At night, before they went to bed, Mama or Joey turned the water off in the cellar in this zero weather, so the pipes would not freeze. But in the day-time there was usually somebody at home, running the water now and then and keeping the fires going.

They heard a trolley coming and hurried to the corner. Joey accidentally stepped on the heel of Jane's rubber and it slid off her shoe, but she managed to slither along on it and they did just barely catch the car. On the trolley it was beautifully warm. In the back of the car some men were smoking and the tobacco smelled good.

"I can stand," said Rufus, for he considered it manly to hang on a strap in trolley cars. Of course he couldn't reach the straps, but he could stand without hanging on. There were seats enough for everybody though, and Mama finally

persuaded him to sit down too. Rufus soon became drowsy and he almost fell asleep. He heard Mama and Joey and Jane talking about the pipes.

"They needn't worry," he told himself. "If the pipes burst, I'll put my finger on the leak the way the boy did in 'The Leak in the Dike.' And I'll hold it there till help comes." He was too sleepy to tell them now. But he certainly was not going to fall asleep on this trolley the way babies do. Every time he felt his head wobble over sideways, he pulled himself up straight with a lurch, and stared at the Drink Moxie ad., or watched the men smoking at the back of the trolley.

Mama and Joey and Jane thought about the pipes. If only they had not burst! It was dreadful to have the pipes burst. The Moffats would have to call a plumber perhaps, and that cost a great deal of money. "Gee," Joey chided himself. "How did I forget?"

"We were all so excited about goin' to the play, we all forgot," said Jane.

"Well, maybe they didn't burst," said Joe. "I stoked the stoves good. That should've kep' the house warm enough."

"Ordinarily it would have," said Mama. "But this is bitter weather. And you know that kind of coal that we get nowadays isn't very good for our stoves."

Soft coal! Bituminous coal! That's the kind of coal they had to burn this year for the good hard nut kind was scarce. When Mama started a fire with this coal what a time she had! "By-two-minutes coal," she called it. "By two minutes the house will be full of smoke," she always said, making a joke of it.

The Moffats hated to get off the trolley where it was so warm. "Why couldn't we live on a trolley?" asked Jane, laughing.

"Sure. We could stretch out on the long seats and sleep," said Joe. "Rufe's practically asleep now."

"I'm not!" denied Rufus, sitting up straight with a jerk. "Just thinkin'. Where are we?"

"Goin' over the Cumberland Avenue bridge," said Jane. They all looked out over the snowy marshes. The sun had set but there was still a wan wintry glow behind the heavy clouds in the west. "Those clouds look like mountains," said Jane. "You could think we were livin' in the mountains."

"That's night comin'," said Joe.

Now the trolley was swaying and sailing up Elm Street. Soon they would have to get off. In the town the streets seemed darker, for the great elm trees and the houses shadowed the sky. Just two more blocks and then they'd be at Ashbellows Place. Rufus was wide awake now and he was the one who pushed the bell. The trolley stopped and the

Moffats stepped out into the cold.

"Br-r-r," said Mama.

The three children raced ahead. They would soon see whether or not the pipes had frozen. They slid up the street on the smooth icy stretches in the gutters, and then they turned into the narrow walk of their own yard. Both sides of the pavement leading to their porch were piled high with great banks of hard snow. "The Grand Canyon!" yelled Jane, her mind still on mountains.

Joey opened the door. The three children stood in the doorway and listened. They didn't hear one thing. This was encouraging, Rufus thought, for if the pipes had burst, surely they would hear water rushing in the cellar. But Joey said no, the pipes might have burst and the water frozen over the break. Or they might have frozen and not burst yet. That would not be quite so bad though, for he and Mama could thaw the pipes themselves with warm cloths and they need not call the plumber.

Joey led the way into the kitchen. Soon he had the lamps lighted. The fire in the stove had gone out! A fire made of this soft coal just did not last and the house was very cold. Catherine-the-cat was sitting right on top of the stove to absorb the last bit of warmth there was in it. Nobody took off his coat or his mittens. And everybody held his breath as Joey went over to the sink. He turned the faucet on. The pipe shuddered but no water came. "Shucks!" said Joe. "It did freeze!" and he quickly turned the spigot off again.

Mama came in now. You could see everybody's breath even though they were in the house. Mama and Joey took the medium-sized lamp and went down to the cellar to investigate. Jane and Rufus stood at the top of the stairs and listened. They could hear Mama and Joey talking in low tones.

"Well," said Rufus, "did they bust?"

There was no answer. Mama and Joey were too busy, tapping the pipes here and feeling them there, to answer. Rufus and Jane stepped cautiously down one or two steps. These stairs did not have any backs to them and were really more like a ladder than a stairway. The unpaved cellar smelled of damp, cold, dirt.

"Did they bust?" Rufus demanded again.

"Yeh," came Joey's muffled voice.

"Bad?" asked Jane.

"No. A little break. Must have just happened," said

Mama.

"Is there goin' to be a flood?" asked Rufus, taking his mitten off and limbering up his forefinger.

"Nope," said Joe. "There's just a little water around the break. Jane, get some things to tie around the pipe."

Jane climbed to the head of the stairs where the rag-bag hung on a nail. But Rufus felt his way up the stairs and into the kitchen and all the way out of the house. Rufus had a plan in his head. It was cold in the Moffats' house. The fire had gone out and the pipes had frozen. It was not at all nice there, thought Rufus. The first thing to do, of course, was to get the pipes fixed. Mama and Joey were taking care of that. The next thing was to fix the stove, but there wasn't anything in the house to start a fire with. And this was where Rufus's plan entered in. He knew of a certain new house that was being built over on Second Avenue. He figured he could get some shavings there to start a fire.

He first snatched an empty burlap bag from the back entry. Then he picked up his red sled, one of the low flat kind with round steel runners. And with his red plaid mackinaw flapping open he took a good run and then belly-flopped across the hard snow that covered the Moffats' lawn

and all the way down the street and across the lot to Elm Street.

In front of the drug store he couldn't resist taking one or two good slides back and forth on the thick green ice that had piled up there. Many colors were reflected in the ice, red and blue ones from the big globes in the drug store window and purple ones from the street lamp. "Well, I better go now and get the wood," said Rufus, and he made ready to take one last good slide.

He ran a way to gain momentum and then he flopped down on his sled. As he was skimming along the ice, his eyes watching the glassy surface go slipping by, he thought he saw something shiny, something shiny frozen in the ice. He thought it looked like money. It looked like a lot of money—not just two cents.

"Probably some old bottle tops," he told himself in order to keep his hopes under control. Nevertheless, he dragged his feet behind him so that he would slow up and he edged his sled backward toward the spot where he thought he had seen something shiny in the ice. He dug his toes and his fingers into the ice getting a grip to pull himself backward. It might have been a mirage such as people see in the desert. They think they see something they want to see, like water or a city, when it isn't really there at all. But he hadn't even been thinking about money. He had been thinking only about getting the wood. Where were the shiny things? Maybe he had imagined them. No! There they were! There they were!

Rufus stopped his sled. He stopped right over the shiny things so he could look at them from between the front runners of his sled. He stared at them for a long, long time. They were money. They were not bottle tops. There were two quarters, three dimes, and two nickels, spread out, frozen solid beneath the surface of the ice. Rufus felt as though he were glued to this spot. He gazed at them, fascinated, taking them in. The coins were there, and they couldn't get away. Nobody else could get them either. He, Rufus, was on top of them on his own sled, nailing them down, laying claim to them like the miners in the Alaska gold fields.

For a long time Rufus was content just to look at the coins. The flickering street lamp made the shadows on the ice ripple like the sea, and Rufus studied the coins as he might study a little school of fish.

"Criminenty!" he murmured. He wiped his nose on the back of his black stocking mitten. "If it's only real," he said.

He closed his eyes for a second. Then he opened them, first one and then the other. The money was still there all right, two nickels, three dimes, and two quarters. And he saw them with both his eyes open and even with just one eye open. He could buy the dinner with this much money, he thought. He laughed to himself when he thought of how surprised all the Moffats would be when he staggered in with a load of food.

"How'm I gonna get it out?" he asked himself.

He didn't have his knife with him. If he went home for it, somebody else might come along, somebody who did have his knife with him, and dig up this money. "Let's see now," he muttered. He'd have to figure some way of getting this gold, this money, out of the ice.

Supposing he left his sled right over it, covering up the spot where the money lay embedded in the ice. No, that was a foolish idea. The sled would just attract attention and, besides, somebody might take his sled into the bargain and he didn't want to lose that. "I know what," he said to himself. He took off his black stocking mitten and tossed it about three yards beyond the money. People would be so busy seeing his mitten and wondering what it was that they wouldn't see the money. "A decoy," he murmured, using a word he had heard Joey say lately.

Rufus hoped he wouldn't lose his mitten either, but certainly with all this much money at stake he would have to risk something. He wondered if he had placed it in the right spot. He backed off a few paces and studied the decoy. Maybe a few inches farther . . . He picked his mitten up, wiped his nose on the back of it again, and again tossed it carelessly down so it would look as though someone really had dropped it. He took one more look at the money. It was safe. It was frozen deeply in the ice and it must have been here for some days. So far no one else had seen it. Now he'd run quickly, get the ice-pick and the chisel, his knife . . . quick . . .

That was what he did. He picked up his sled and tore. He belly-flopped up the street and across the empty lot so fast he didn't see Mr. Price coming until he was right up to him. Mr. Price had to leap into the air to avoid being knocked down.

MONEY IN THE ICE

When Rufus reached home, he could hear Mama and Joey still banging pipes down in the cellar. Janey was shaking down the cold ashes in the kitchen range, getting it ready for a new fire.

"I'll bring home some wood in a minute," Rufus yelled at her as he banged out of the house with the chisel and his knife. All the while he kept asking himself, "Are they safe?"

Fortunately it was really very dark now, although the lights in the drug store window cast a glow that lighted up Rufus's mitten. Nobody had taken that anyway. If only nobody had taken the money. "Be there! Be there!" Rufus ordered, hardly daring to look. Now here was where the money should be, and here it was! Here it was! The same thing—two quarters, three dimes, and a couple of nickels. No one else had seen them. Rufus sat on his sled and he scraped and dug, chipped and filed, and finally he had them all out. He warmed the coins in his chubby, chapped fist.

While Rufus was standing in the red glow from the window, warming his money, Spec Cullom, the ice-man, came along. What luck for him, out of all the people in Cranbury, to be the one to come along right now! Because in the winter time Spec Cullom was also a plumber as well as the ice-man. Not many people bought ice in the winter time and a great many people needed help with their water pipes at this season. He had his plumbing kit with him right now, as a matter of fact. He stepped into the drug store. Rufus heard him ask for a package of Bull Durham tobacco before he was inside the door.

Rufus waited for Spec Cullom to come out. Rufus remembered the day the ice-man had given him an empty Bull Durham tobacco pouch. "Here, fella," he had said. "Put this in your pocket." Rufus kept it there along with the postcard from the soldier named Al. It gave his pocket a faint smell of tobacco that he liked. Rufus looked in the drug store window. The ice-man was drinking a soda. Then he came out and he saw Rufus.

"Hello, fella," he said, starting to spar around a bit.

Rufus didn't spar back this time. His fist was full of money wanting to be spent. "Look," he said, wiping his nose on his sleeve. "I dug this up out of the ice."

"Lucky fella," said Spec Cullom, shoving his hat back on his head.

"How much of this money would it take to fix our pipe?

It busted," said Rufus.

Spec rolled a cigarette, wetting the edge of it down with his tongue. "How much do you think it's worth?" he asked.

Rufus looked at his money, studying what he was going to do with each piece. It was worth more than a nickel to have pipes fixed. He knew that. If he gave Spec one of the big pieces he might not have enough left to buy the supper. However, a pipe is important. He held up one of the quarters and looked up at him anxiously.

But Spec shook his head. Reluctantly Rufus added the other quarter. Now he could buy hardly any supper. But Spec Cullom shook his head in disgust. "Five cents does it, fella," he said.

"A nickel?" asked Rufus incredulously. He picked one of these coins out and gave it to the ice-man.

"That does it," said Spec, and he flipped the coin in the air, caught it, and stuck it in his pocket. "I'll drop right over," he added.

"Will you tell Mama I paid already?" asked Rufus.

"Right, Boss. So long!" And he winked at Rufus and hastened up the street with a careless, loose stride.

"S'long." said Rufus, looking after him admiringly and smiling to himself.

Then he crossed the street to the grocery store with as loose and careless a gait as he could muster with a sled to pull. Rufus laid all his money on the counter. He bought two packages of kindling wood, for of course he had given up the idea of going way over to Second Avenue after all that had happened. He bought a small sackful of good, hard nut coal. "Not that soft by-two-minutes kind," he said. "We have some of that." He bought some apples, some oranges, some eggs, and some potatoes, and he went home feeling like Santa Claus.

This time when he reached home Mama and Joey were in the kitchen too. Somebody else was down in the cellar, bang-banging at the pipes, and Rufus knew who that was. Spec Cullom!

Joey and Mama had to heat some water to thaw out the pipes. "Now what am I goin' to start this old fire with?" Joey asked in perplexity. And right then was the time for Rufus to drag in his sledful of treasures.

"I found the money in the ice!" he yelled, jumping up and down so hard that Spec Cullom came dashing up the stairs to see what was wrong now.

Joey lost no time in making the fires, and Mama heated the water to thaw the pipes. It wasn't long before Spec had the break soldered together and then Mama went to the faucet to turn on the water.

Cr-unch! Cr-eak! Cr-rack! The water was trying to come through the ice. Then with terrific spasms that shook the faucet the water did burst out of the pipe, first in rusty spurts and then in a good clear stream!

Spec Cullom left and Mama started to cook the supper. She made lots of apple fritters, using the supplies that Rufus had brought home. "Tell it again!" first one and then another asked Rufus. And he had to tell again the whole story of how he had found the money in the ice.

Naturally all the Moffats were excited about it.

"Imagine finding so much money in the ice!" marveled Jane, and she slid over the ice very carefully for some days, hoping she too would find a treasure. As for Rufus, he was the happiest of all. He went to bed that night right after supper, thinking about his luck. Finding the money in the ice more than made up for the disappointment about the Indians. He really felt like a hero. He hadn't had to hold his finger in the leak in the pipe. But he had come home with the money and everybody had had a good dinner. Furthermore, now the house was good and warm.

8

RUFUS'S BEANS

RUFUS SAT IN THE THIRD SEAT IN THE THIRD ROW IN ROOM Three. His head was bent low over his arithmetic paper. He was trying to find the least common denominator. He heard someone come into the classroom and he looked up thinking more about how he could make six go into four than about who was at the door. Then he jumped and almost upset his inkwell. There was Mama walking across the front of the room from the door to the teacher's desk with those short hurried steps of hers. Rufus was really shocked. Here was Mama in Room Three! "Am I crazy?" thought Rufus. He closed his eyes and then opened them again, half expecting the apparition of Mama in the schoolroom to disappear while he had them shut.

But it didn't. Mama was at the desk now. She said something in a low voice to the teacher. Then she turned her head, took in the room with a quick glance, found Rufus, smiled at him, and hurried out.

Well! Rufus bent his head very low over his arithmetic paper again. The boy across the aisle, Hughie Pudge, whispered, "Hey, Rufe, that was your mother." And the whole class looked at Rufus. After a while they stopped looking, for Rufus kept his eyes right on his arithmetic paper. Mama had come into Room Three. All right. What of it? That's the way he was trying to act.

Once he had seen Mama come walking across the Green. That time if he had been thinking where Mama was he'd have thought she was at home in the kitchen. But he hadn't been thinking and suddenly he happened to meet her on the Green. He was quite taken aback that time. Away from home Mama looked so familiar and yet like someone you didn't know too. But to see Mama come into Room Three in the middle of the arithmetic lesson was even more of a shock than seeing her come across the Green in her blue suit.

The morning wore on. Fractions gave way to spelling, spelling to reading "By the Shores of Gitche Gumee," Gitche Gumee to singing "Hats Off, Hats Off, the Flag is Passing By," and, when school was dismissed, Rufus was still asking himself why Mama had come into the school-room.

The teacher called Rufus to the desk and told him Mama had left a message for him. She and Sylvie had had to go to New York unexpectedly, and Jane's and Joey's teachers had been told this too, and they were all to play around the house and not roam all over town. Jane was going to fix the lunch and the supper.

Jane was waiting for Rufus, Joey was waiting for both of them, and Nancy was waiting for Jane, so they all walked up the street together, talking excitedly about how Mama had gone into every room where there was a Moffat.

"Why'd they have to go to New York?" Rufus finally thought to ask.

Whenever Mama had gone to New York in the past she

had prepared for the excursion a long time in advance. She would take some of Sylvie's programs, an example of Rufus's left-handed writing, one of Joey's good Latin papers, and a robin drawn by Jane. Everything to show the people in New York what four smart children she had.

"Yes," said Jane. "And why do you think they went all of a sudden?"

"Probably wanted to go to the zoo," Rufus speculated.

"Aw, zoo nothin'," said Joey. "Said she had to go to New York to see Tonty. She's sick. She sent Mama the tickets for her and Sylvie. Special delivery."

"Oh," said Rufus. Tonty was Mama's sister and she lived in New York. All the Moffats had been to New York at least once to see Tonty.

"Gee," said Jane. "I hope Mama and Sylvie don't fall into the hands of counterfeiters, the way they sometimes do in books."

"Aw, they wouldn't," said Rufus in disgust. "They know money from paper."

"It doesn't matter if they know money from paper," said Jane. "What they have to know is regular people from counterfeiters, so they don't fall into their hands."

"I wonder if they'll go to the Hippodrome," said Nancy. "I went there once. Saw elephants on the stage. Well, so long," she said, turning into her house.

"So long," said Jane and Joe and Rufus, and they crawled through the gate in the fence that separated their yard from Nancy's and went home to lunch.

Mama had left some lentil soup for them on the stove. They ate it and while they were eating Jane said, "Listen! Let's be good to Mama. The minute she says to any one of us, 'Go to the store,' we'll go. We won't say, 'Aw, you go, Rufe,' or 'You go, Joe.' Whoever she asks to go, that person, *go!*"

"Yeh," said Joe.

Rufus was busy scraping his plate clean, but with the spoon in his mouth he nodded his head up and down too.

They all felt good, full of fine intentions, and then they all went back to school.

Rufus hung his hat in the cloak room on peg three. He went into the schoolroom and sat down in his seat. The first thing this class did in the afternoon was geography.

"Where does the river Penobscot rise?" the teacher asked. "Hands?"

A lot of hands were raised, but before the teacher could call on anybody the door opened and a man came into the schoolroom. This was not the music supervisor, the writing supervisor, nor the Superintendent of Schools. And this was not a soldier to tell some of his experiences. This was an ordinary man. Mama had come into the classroom earlier Maybe this was somebody's father. But he wasn't. He was a man who started right in talking about gardens.

Everybody in the class should raise a Victory Garden, he said; plant seeds and raise vegetables, so this country would have food enough for the armed forces and the stricken nations, and thus help win the war. He stated that he would go up one street and down another teaching the people how to plant their gardens and how to take care of them. "My name is Hogan," he said. "Be looking for me.

I'll be there." And he left.

The man's plan sounded good to Rufus. In the past the four Moffats had planted small gardens and sometimes they had had real radishes, carrots, and lettuce from them that they could eat. He could hardly wait to get home and start his Victory Garden, especially after the teacher passed around bright packages of vegetable seeds to all the children. They were two cents a package and the children could bring the pennies for them any time during the week. Rufus chose beans, string beans.

When school was out, Joey and Jane met Rufus again. Nancy Stokes ran up. Everybody in the school yard was talking about the man. Rufus found that he had been in every room telling everybody about Victory Gardens. Joe and Jane and Nancy had bright packages of seeds too. But they were not supposed to plant them until the man came to their house, looked their yard over, and gave advice.

The children hurried home as fast as they could. The man might come to their house first. They sat down on the front porch and waited for the man. "My name is Hogan," he'd said in every room. "I'll be there," he'd said. The Moffats waited for him but he didn't come. They waited at least fifteen minutes, jumping up every few seconds and running to the street to look for him. They hoped that by now he was at least next door. But no, he was nowhere in sight. They grew tired of waiting. Of course, they reasoned, the man couldn't be everywhere at once. He probably began over on the other side of town or up on Shingle Hill. Why wait for this man any longer? They knew how to plant gardens—dig up the earth, pick out the chunks, the roots, the rocks, and the boulders, drop in the seeds, water everything, cover up the seeds, pat the earth down, put up signs telling what was planted where, and let it grow.

Why wait for this man any longer, they asked themselves again, running to the corner and giving him one last chance. At this rate spring would be over and summer gone while they sat here and waited for a man to show them how to plant. That man was good for people who did not know how to plant, they decided, but they did know how. Moreover, consider the nice surprise for Mama and Sylvie when they returned tonight to know the gardens had been planted!

Rufus was the most impatient. He looked at his big fat envelope of beans. Lovely bright green vines and beans were

painted on the cover. "Wait, if you want to, for the man,"
he said. "I'm diggin' now."

"Me too," agreed Jane. "Mama will be glad we worked
while she was away and did not gallivant."

The Moffats' back yard was very small. Their front yard
was very long. What a vegetable garden they could plant in
the front yard, the children thought! But then they would
have to dig up all that green grass, and, besides, they had
never seen a vegetable garden in anybody's front yard; only
flowers. They'd better begin on the back yard, especially as
Mama was away and they could not ask her what she
thought. Maybe later she would let them plant the whole
front yard too.

Joey took a stick and marked off a square. There was no
grass in this square, just hard dirt, pounded down by children playing games here, especially hopscotch. Then Joey
marked the square off into four sections, one each for all
four Moffats.

"We'll dig a space for Sylvie too," he said. "Most likely
she'd like to plant something, radishes perhaps."

Sylvie liked radishes. Not Rufus. He liked beans. He was
going to plant nothing but beans. The beans were big and

he could see them when he stuck them in the ground. He examined Joey's onion seed to see if that was going to be fun. No, they weren't any good—tiny little things. "What's the good of onion seeds?" thought Rufus. These big white beans of his, one by one . . . He could hardly wait for the digging part of the Victory Gardens to be finished.

"Everybody plant beans," he urged.

Jane did not want to plant beans. She liked corn better. If Rufus were going to plant only beans, the rest of them should plant other vegetables so they would not have to eat beans all the time. Naturally since corn on the cob was Jane's favorite vegetable, corn was what she was going to plant.

"Do you know how to plant it?" asked Nancy, as she crawled through the gate in the fence with some extra spades and shovels.

"Yes," said Jane. "I watched a man in the country plant corn once. He was a real farmer. He planted the corn in little hills. Or, rather, I can't quite remember whether he planted the corn up in the little hills he made or down in the little holes beside the hills."

"I should think up in the hills," said Nancy, "so they'd get the sun."

"Yeh," said Jane. "But down in the little valleys the water would collect whenever it rained and keep them nice and wet."

'That's so too," agreed Nancy.

"Still, I'm not sure," said Jane. And all the while she and Nancy dug, they discussed the pros and cons of planting the corn down in the little hollows or up on the mounds.

Rufus dug hard. His hands and face were red. He didn't talk to anybody. He was anxious to get his beans into the ground as rapidly as possible and watch them grow. Joey did not talk much either. He was figuring in his mind about this back yard. This garden they were planting would use up most of the space. But there would still be room in the old barn for silver foxes if he started to raise them. That ad. about silver foxes was still running in *Popular Mechanics*.

Finally the children finished digging. Joey measured out the little furrows where the seeds should be dropped. He did not measure out Jane's corn patch. She had to do those special hills and valleys herself. Joey felt like a real surveyor with a piece of string tied to two sticks. He held one and

Rufus the other, and they drew a line where each groove for the seeds should be made.

Then Rufus placed his beans, one by one, carefully in his three furrows. The beans were very pretty, standing out white against the dark brown earth. Rufus liked the smell of the earth. He patted it down good and hard over his beans and he left loose dirt in the paths to walk on. Joey said this was wrong. The earth should be scattered loosely over the seeds and patted down hard on the paths. This did not seem natural to Rufus, for it is much pleasanter to walk on soft dirt and one can easily see where the beans lie if the dirt is patted down hard on them. Nevertheless he did as Joey said.

Rufus watched Joey sprinkle onion seed and carrot seed in his space. And he watched Jane and Nancy deliberately stick their corn kernels down in the little valleys where they finally decided to plant them. "Next to beans, corns are the best things to plant," thought Rufus, "because you can see them good too."

Finally everybody had all his seeds planted. The children were really tired now. They stuck a shingle at the end of each row and put the empty seed envelopes on them. Now

everything was properly labeled and no one would confuse the carrots with the beans. As though that were possible, thought Rufus, who knew he would never forget exactly where his three rows of beans were planted; and he gazed at these fondly.

The children had worked so hard they were certainly hungry now. Nancy ran home to supper and Jane heated the rest of the lentil soup. She and Joey and Rufus ate this and then they went out on the front porch and sat down to wait for Mama and Sylvie.

Every now and then Rufus ran around to the back yard, went straight to his bean patch, and looked to see if any of his beans were up yet. It began to grow dark. The darker it grew, the closer to the earth Rufus had to crouch. He even lay flat on his stomach and examined the earth to see if just one of his beans might not have started to grow. Finally he gently poked his earth-stained forefinger into the soft ground, felt around carefully, and found a bean. He pulled it out, held it between his fingers, rolled it on his palm, and studied it. It looked just the same as when he planted it a little while before. Only its skin looked a little shriveled.

Rufus put it back and covered it up and patted down the earth.

"Grow." he said.

On the front porch Joe said to Jane, "Rufus expects his beans to be up already."

"I know it," laughed Jane.

As a matter of fact Jane was having to hug her knees to keep from running around to her corn mounds just to make sure some of that wasn't beginning to sprout too. She closed her eyes happily as she envisioned tall corn blowing in the breeze and herself reaching up on tiptoes to pick enough ears for supper. She liked corn so much, golden bantam corn, that as far as she was concerned the family could have it for breakfast, lunch, and dinner. In fact she wouldn't mind having a corn week. Last winter one week had been set aside as potato week when everybody was supposed to eat as many potatoes as possible. The Moffats had had potato pancakes often. It was lucky there was never a squash week, for nobody was very fond of that. But corn week! That would be the best of all, thought Jane.

"I better see what Rufus is doin'," said Jane. "He might be stepping on the seeds."

"Yeh," agreed Joe.

Rufus picked himself up when he heard Jane. He said, "Nothin's up yet."

"O' course not," said Jane.

After Rufus disappeared around the house, Jane stood surveying her corn patch. Had she been right in putting the corn down in the little valleys or should she have planted it up in the hills? She finally bent over, poked her finger around in the dirt until she found a kernel, held it up, and examined it. It did not look any different than it had when she planted it. She stuck it back in the earth and rejoined the others.

"Nothin's up yet," she said.

Joey had been thinking about his onions. There was one thing everybody in the Moffats' house liked very much and that was pot roast and onions. Onions were very important. In fact, Joey was sure a day scarcely ever went by when Mama did not need an onion.

Of course nothing was up yet, he thought. You could excuse Rufus for thinking things were up because he was so little, but Jane should know better. Onion seeds were so small, Joey thought, that you probably couldn't even see them now any more. He wondered if you could. If you could still see them, he wondered what they'd look like— same as they always looked probably.

Janey and Rufus raced down to the corner to watch the trolleys and wait for Mama. While they were gone, Joey sauntered around to the back yard and looked at the garden. This was a good garden they'd planted. Just for the fun of it, why not see what onion seed looked like now? He dug around with his fingers in the onion row. He couldn't see any seed at all. It was getting pretty dark now. Perhaps if he had a match . . .

Joey went into the kitchen, found a match, lighted it on his corduroy pants, and held it close to the ground. He couldn't see a trace of the seed. He hoped the ants hadn't eaten them—if they ate onion seed. Of course the onions hadn't started to grow yet and neither had Jane's corn nor Rufus's beans. Rufus and Jane were crazy to even think anything might have come up!

Joey went into the kitchen again for a drink of water. He found a glass and smelled it, as he always did before drinking. Once he had taken a drink of water out of a glass that had had kerosene oil spilled in it. He wasn't taking any more chances of drinking water out of glasses that smelled like kerosene. He drank a couple of glasses of water and looked at the clock. Half-past seven. He put a little coal in the kitchen range, shook the ashes down, and poked a good draft in the red coals. Then he looked around to see if there were any apples. There weren't. There were only onions in a brown bag. Joey took out one onion and looked at it. Soon Mama would not have to buy any more onions. They'd have his onions. Then Joey had an idea. He stuck the onion in his pocket and ran out of the house.

"Hey, Rufe . . . Jane!" he yelled. "Come 'ere!"

Rufus and Jane came racing home. "What's the matter?"

"Hey," said Joe. "Look at my onion!" He waved the full-grown onion at them.

Jane and Rufus stopped short. What was this, a whole onion already? They stared, stunned, not quite believing. If a whole onion had grown, then where were their beans and corn?

"Criminenty!" shouted Rufus with a whoop. "I bet my beans are up!" and he tore around back with Jane and Joe after him.

"That's not a real onion," Jane accused Joe.

" 'Tis so," said Joe.

"Didn't come out of your garden, I bet," said Jane.

"Where'd it come from then?" countered Joe.

"It's too big." Jane felt she might believe a small onion but not this big one. Still, how could she be sure? She joined Rufus, who had flung himself down on his stomach again, looking for a crack in the earth at least, where a bean might be emerging.

"Grow, beans," he begged.

The back yard was much darker than the front now, for it was hemmed in by apple trees, fences, and the barn. Now they really could not see any more. With a sigh Rufus stood up. "My beans ain't up," he said sadly.

They went into the house with Rufus thoroughly believing in Joey's onion, though Jane still felt somewhat skeptical. Joey lighted the lamps and they all sat around the kitchen table waiting for Mama and Sylvie. Joey took the newspaper, spread it out on the red checked tablecloth, and started to read the war news. Jane got out her paper and her paints and began to make some paper dolls.

Rufus just sat at the table and thought about his beans. "I'll have to get bean poles," he said.

"Yeh," said Joey, "we'll make 'em tomorrow."

"Maybe it was because we didn't plant any bean poles with the beans that my beans didn't grow like your onion," said Rufus.

Joey felt sorry for Rufus. He decided he had carried his joke far enough. "Aw," he said, "I was foolin' about the onion."

When Rufus understood the joke, he thought it was a pretty good one. However, he was not absolutely certain it was a joke and he still felt his beans should be up by now. It seemed a long, long time since he had stuck those beans in the dirt. He laid his head on his arm, listened to the crackling of Joey's newspaper, and smelled the ink of the print.

Beans! He thought of them climbing bean poles to the sky, or at least as far as the beans in "Jack-the-Giant-Killer." Beans to keep the Moffats supplied the whole year. Beans for an army. That's the kind of Victory Garden Rufus had planted and he wanted to see the results.

Rufus grew sleepier and sleepier. The newspaper crackled with a comfortable sound. He wished he could go out and take one last look at his beans. But it was pitch black now.

Catherine-the-cat sat disconsolately in the window sill, looking out. She knew Mama was away and she did not like this.

Jane cut out paper dolls for a time and then she, too, laid her head on her arm and watched the lamp flicker every time Joey turned a page. Whenever she heard a train, she said, "Maybe they're on that."

"Maybe," said Joe.

Then Rufus really fell asleep. Joey thought of carrying him upstairs to bed. Then he decided not to. He liked Rufus's company even though he was asleep. Jane didn't really fall all the way asleep. But she only half heard Joey shovel coal on the stove and shake down the ashes, and she only half heard drops of rain spattering on the window, and Joey murmur, "Now it's rainin'. Wish they'd come now." And Jane thought of all the little corn valleys filling up with water and hoped she and Nancy had planted right. . . .

The next thing Jane and Rufus knew, Mama and Sylvie had walked up on the porch, come into the house, and there they were, standing beside the kitchen stove, warming their hands and drying themselves. Jane and Rufus waked right up and Mama made some hot cocoa out of evaporated milk. And while she was making the cocoa she was talking.

". . . And Tonty is much better and wasn't it nice of her to send us tickets to come and see her? They came by special delivery."

"Special delivery," thought Rufus. "I got a card once in Room Three. Not special delivery though . . ."

Joey and Jane and Rufus were so excited about seeing Mama and Sylvie home from their travels they forgot about their gardens. Yes, even Rufus forgot about his beans and went to bed.

But the minute Rufus waked up in the morning he remembered. "My beans!" he cried, and rushed out the door before he had eaten his oatmeal. Although the ground was still damp, he flopped down on his stomach and examined his bean plot. The raindrops had stepped all over the garden leaving tiny holes on planted places and paths alike. "It's lucky we stuck the names of the seeds on those sticks or we wouldn't know where's onions and where's carrots," thought Rufus.

As for him, he knew exactly where his beans were because his plot was at one end of the garden. He put his finger in the wet earth and felt around gently. Where was that bean? Ah, here it was. He lifted it out tenderly and studied it. The bean still looked the way it had yesterday. No, it was possibly a little more shriveled, he thought. But that was the only difference.

Every day thereafter, several times during the day, Rufus flopped down close to the earth and watched for his beans. What he hoped was that he would be right there, watching, when the first bean popped out of the ground.

Mama said to him, "A watched pot never boils."

"These ain't pots," said Rufus. "These are beans."

And he kept watching. The one bean in particular that he was watching he had taken out of the earth several times now. Today he felt around for it as usual. Now he found it and pulled it out.

"Zowie!" he exclaimed. "What's this?" The bean had a little sprout growing from it, like a little piece of string. Rufus became very happy. "My bean's growin'," he said proudly to Jane.

"Put it back! Put it back!" she screamed. "It's growin'," and she dug feverishly for a corn kernel to see if it too was growing.

Rufus put his bean back in the soil. He secretly dug up one bean after another to see whether they all had little strings attached to them. Most of them did. He ran to school feeling very encouraged about his Victory Garden. Jane sighed. Her corn! Not a sprout was visible on it, and the kernels had taken on a rather brown old look. Had she planted them right? Valleys or hills? Where was the man named Hogan? If hills were right, perhaps she should take the corn out of the valleys and put them in the mounds. Then she heard Nancy whistle and she dashed through the gate in the fence and joined her best friend.

This was a very warm day and it grew warmer and warmer as the afternoon wore on. In school the windows were flung wide open. The doors were kept open too and you could hear children in the different classrooms reciting. Sometimes a teacher raised her voice scoldingly. Goodness! It was actually hot! The children began to count how many weeks before vacation. Too many, they thought desperately. It really was terribly hot. It felt like the middle of summer and it was only the beginning of May. Yesterday the buds on the trees could hardly be seen. Today the leaves were out, tiny and green.

None of the children wore their coats home. They slung them over their shoulders and trudged along. Not Rufus. He never trudged. He always ran, even on hot days like this, and particularly ever since he had planted his beans.

He was the first one of the Moffats home and he ran right over to his bean patch. Before he got there he knew it! He knew it! His beans were up! There were crooked cracks in the earth and a split pale-green leaf wherever he had planted a bean.

"Mama," he yelled exultantly, "come 'ere! My beans! My beans are growin'. They're up! They're up!"

That's the way it was. Of all the seeds, Rufus's beans were the first to sprout. The man who was supposed to say "Plant this way and that way" never did get around to the Moffats' house. In time Jane decided she must have planted her corn the wrong way. Joey's onions and carrots came up in even, green rows. Sylvie had planted lettuce and it grew nicely. Janey's corn finally did come up but it never grew very high. It did look pretty, but the Moffats never got so much as one ear of corn to eat from it. "Hills, not valleys, is the way to plant corn," she informed Nancy Stokes.

But Rufus's beans! They grew, all right. They climbed

the poles. Lots of daddy-long-legs came to live among the vines. And not only did the Moffats have green beans for dinner all summer, they let one row of beans dry on the vines and by winter had a sackful of dried beans.

And they never said, "We're going to have beans for supper," or, "Pass the beans, please." They always said, "We're going to have Rufus's beans for supper," or, "Pass me some Rufus beans, please." That's what they always said.

9

FIREWORKS AND BURIED TREASURE

ON THE FOURTH OF JULY RUFUS WAS SITTING ON THE bottom step of the porch burning a piece of punk, the only thing he had left of his fireworks. Not that punk is really fireworks, but at least it burned. It was better than nothing and, besides, it kept mosquitoes away. Joey had fired off his last giant firecracker and Jane had watched her last snake wind out of its little capsule. Everybody was glad that Sylvie liked night fireworks the best and had spent all her money on pinwheels and Roman candles. Otherwise the Fourth of July would be over and it was only nine o'clock in the morning.

Usually Rufus did not want the night-time to come because night meant bedtime. But today he wished it would hurry up, so they could shoot the Roman candles and the skyrockets. He burned his punk and he looked longingly at the night works. They were in a shoe box in a corner of the porch all ready to be set off. Beside the pink and green and blue skyrockets and Roman candles there was a box of sparklers, practically full. The children had burned one last night just to see how it looked.

Rufus watched his punk and the wisp of smoke winding away from it. It smelled good but punk is rather tiresome. It doesn't flare up into anything big and bright. It just smolders. Still Rufus burned his punk waiting for the night-time.

Rufus did not like to wait for night-time or for anything else. Sometimes, when he went walking with Mama in the evening, she'd stop to talk with some lady around the corner. Rufus would stand first on one foot and then on the other. He would tug on Mama's skirt every now and then, a gentle reminder that he was still there, that he was tired, that he wanted to go home, and finally that he didn't like to stand there while she was talking. But talk, talk, Mama and the lady talked and talked.

Now he burned his punk and he waited. "Come, night-time," he urged impatiently.

Jane came skipping around the house.

"What time is it?" Rufus asked her.

"About nine o'clock," she said.

"What time does it get dark at night?"

"About nine."

Rufus groaned.

"How'm I gonna wait?" he asked.

Mama came out of the house and sat down in the little green rocker to sew. She moved into the shade cast by the hop-vines and said, "Gracious, today is going to be a scorcher."

"Do we have to wait till it's pitch black for the night works?" Rufus asked.

"Of course," said Mama, fanning herself with a palm leaf fan. She studied Rufus's despondent little back for a while. Then she said,

"Why don't you and Jane and Joey go over to Sandy Beach for the day? You could take some sandwiches."

"Whoops!" Jane and Rufus tore all over the house like

Indians, throwing off their clothes, putting on their bathing suits, and yelling for Joey. Sylvie helped make the sandwiches. Cheese sandwiches they were, snappy cheese, and Jane packed them in a box with some apples. Sylvie said she wished she could go too but she had to get ready for tonight. Jack Abbot said he might come over, and she wanted to shampoo her hair.

"Good-by," she and Mama called as the three youngest Moffats ran barefoot across the grass, heavy coats slung over their arms, for they would be practically frozen coming home, dripping wet, with their teeth chattering no matter how hot the day was.

"Come home when you see the *Richard Peck*," added Mama.

"All right! All right! Good-by! Good-by!"

The *Richard Peck* was the steamboat that ran between New York and New Haven and it sailed into the harbor at four o'clock on Sundays and holidays.

Well! Rufus was glad. They would swim all day and then they would have supper and soon after that they could light the night works.

He and Jane and Joe ran across the lot, their bare heels

pounding the hard dirt path and their arms waving the grasshoppers and dragonflies out of the way.

When they reached Elm Street, they slowed down to a walk. The trolleys were so crowded with excursionists that some were hanging on the running boards, screaming and laughing and blowing tin horns, all on their way to the beaches for the holiday. There were too many automobiles on the road to play the game they had made up of "This is my car and this is yours." Often they sat on the corner on Sunday afternoons and watched the autos go past and the first would be Joey's and the next Jane's and the next Rufus's and then Joey's again.

"Boy, oh, boy," Joey would say when he got a beautiful long red car. And everybody would yell derisively when Jane got one dilapidated old tin lizzie after another the whole afternoon.

Now and then they stopped to watch a boy set off a giant firecracker. And again Rufus and Joey wished they had some more day works. However, once they reached Sandy Beach, they all began to forget about firecrackers, for these were not permitted here. Only once in a while from a distance they heard a torpedo and a bang reminding them it was still the Fourth of July. They put their coats and lunch box in the shade under a crab-apple tree far up on the beach and now they were ready for a swim.

Rufus thought he could swim. All winter he had been thinking he could swim because the last time he went in swimming last summer he had actually swum five strokes without water wings, logs, or anything. Now, splashing around in the water, he found he was mistaken. He could not swim. Jane, standing shivering ankle-deep, assured him swimming was like bicycle riding. Once you knew how you knew how for life. He'd soon get the hang of it again. And with these encouraging words she plunged in bravely, hoping the theory would work with her likewise. Joey had already swum way out to the raft and was doing the jack-knife, the swan, and all kinds of dives.

Rufus and Jane splashed around vigorously, did dead man's float, ducked with eyes open and eyes closed, tried under-water swimming, dove for rocks in the shallow water, and finally, completely water-soaked, with eyes pink and lips blue, they flopped in the hot sand to warm up. They gathered sea-shells and Rufus put them in a grubby old cigarette box he found for the Moffats' museum, as they now called the barn.

It was then that Jane got the idea they should bury treasure.

"Let's play pirates," she suggested. "I'm Cap'n Blackbeard. You're my man, Bloody Jim."

"Right," said Rufus, not minding Jane's being the captain since he had such a good name and, anyway, the game was her idea.

"Come on," said Jane. "We'll bury treasure, mark the spot with a stick, and when Joey comes back we'll dig it up and surprise him."

This idea appealed to Rufus. "It will get even with him for pulling up that onion that time in his Victory Garden," he said energetically.

They dug a hole in the sand above the high water line. The captain paced off the distance. Ten feet from the gnarly crab-apple tree, three feet above the high water mark, and two feet from a deserted little boathouse.

"Now what'll we bury?" asked Rufus. The hole was dug, gaping in the sand waiting for the treasure.

Jane thought a moment. "Valuables. My little blue ring for one."

Louis Slobodkin

"The one Tonty sent you from New York?" asked Rufus incredulously.

"Of course. Treasure is treasure," said Jane, dropping her ring into the hole. "What have you got? Speak up, Bloody Jim."

"Nuthin'," came the tough answer of the assistant pirate.

"Nuthin'!" exclaimed Cap'n Blackbeard.

"Well," said Bloody Jim after a thoughtful pause as he considered the possibilities. Since they had come in their bathing suits, naturally they were not very well equipped with treasure. "There's my shells," and he dropped in the grimy box with the delicate little shells.

"All right. What else?" demanded Cap'n Blackbeard.

"That's all the valuables I got, Cap'n."

"Men have died for less than that, Bloody Jim. How about that signet ring on your little finger?"

"Won't come off, Cap'n. Honest," said the man, Bloody Jim, with an appropriate whine.

"Lessee!" The captain's voice boded ill.

Bloody Jim held out his chubby fist. The captain coaxed and pulled at the ring. No use. The ring was on to stay.

"How are you ever goin' to get that off?" A momentary

lapse into Janey Moffat's own voice.

"Old Natby the blacksmith'll file it off," replied Rufus in his regular Rufus voice.

But now harsh sounded the voice of Captain Blackbeard. "You'll hang for the next offense. For the present keep your ring," he said, flinging the hand of Bloody Jim from him in high dudgeon. "And consider yourself lucky I don't saw off your finger," he added.

"Aye, aye, sir."

"Fill in the hole. Be quick about it."

"Aye, aye, sir."

Then the captain marked the spot and the buried treasure was ready to be dug up as soon as Joey came back. And here was Joey now. But Jane and Rufus forgot about the treasure when Joey said,

"Come on, Rufe and Jane! A fellow said he'd take us for a row. He's in my Naval Reserve."

"O-o-o-h! Swell!" said Jane, and they all ran for their coats and their lunch. Then they went back to the water's edge to wait for the boy.

"Here he comes," said Joe.

A big boy in a small red boat rowed skillfully to shore.

"What a beaut!" said Rufus, and the three Moffats climbed aboard. Jane sat in the back seat with her feet overboard in the cool green water. As she watched the shore line grow farther and farther away, she suddenly remembered the buried treasure. Her finger missed the little blue ring. Well, the game of digging it up and surprising Jocy would have to wait until they got back. The way the tide was coming in, it was lucky she knew enough to plant the treasure above the high water mark.

The three Moffats didn't say much. They just watched the scenery change. Now they were way out by the raft, and now they had passed it and were heading for the coal barge. Now they had reached the coal barge, and the only way they could distinguish Sandy Beach was by the large crowd of children there. The boathouses looked like toy houses and the shouts from the raft sounded miles away. Maybe Joe's friend was going to row them under the Cumberland Avenue bridge. All the Moffats hoped so.

"I'll row if you get tired," Rufus offered shyly. But the boy didn't hear him. Rufus spoke a little louder.

". . . Row if you get tired," he suggested. The boy heard him this time.

"Right," said the boy. "Soon's we get through the bridge the job is yours."

Rufus smiled and sat in readiness to take over. Now they were going under the bridge. They couldn't help ducking though there really was plenty of room between them and the bridge. And now here they were in the river beyond. It wound its way through the high grass of the marshes. Dragonflies and horseflies darted over their heads. An occasional sea gull swooped ahead of them into the river for a fish. And schools of little fish scattered hither and thither at this intrusion into their quiet waters.

Rufus took the oars and the Moffats began to feel at home in this boat and with this big boy. They began to sing.

> "Row, row, row the boat
> Gently down the stream,
> Merrily, merrily, merrily, merrily,
> Life is but a dream."

They sang it over and over, that is, all of them but Rufus. He was working very hard at the oars. Occasionally an oar slipped out of his hand, his right hand. And it would have gone sailing down the river had not Joey's friend quickly

retrieved it. So Joey sat beside him and took one of the oars and pulled with Rufus. And they pulled up the river to the next bend. The water was rising quickly and spreading over the marsh. The children rested now and ate their sandwiches, sharing them with Joey's friend.

"Goodness!" said Jane. "How high the tide is getting!"

"Sure," said Joe. "Today is perigee tide."

"Perigee tide! What's that?" asked Jane.

"Well . . . it's an unusually high tide."

"Oh," said Jane, clasping her finger where her ring was supposed to be and with dismay clutching at her heart.

"Why? What's the matter?" asked Joe.

"Oh . . . nothing. But . . . how much higher does this pedigree tide come than the regular everyday one?"

"Way up. Covers the whole of Sandy Beach. Sometimes reaches way up to the bushes," put in Joey's friend as he again took the oars.

"It does?" gasped Jane. And she tried to catch Rufus's eye. But he was watching how with each pull the fellow almost yanked the oar lock out of the boat but never did quite. If he did, who'd dive for it, Joey or the big boy? Rufus couldn't. Not yet. Maybe by the time they had to go home, he'd have learned to dive. Swim and dive, both.

Jane did not enjoy the last part of the row. They were going back under the Cumberland Avenue bridge now and everybody really had to stoop this time in order not to bump their heads, for the water had risen so. Now they were back in the harbor and Jane kept straining her eyes for a glimpse of the shore line. At last she could distinguish Sandy Beach and, yes, the water had rolled way up onto the shore. There was almost no Sandy Beach at all. When the boat scraped the bottom, she breathed a hurried "Thank you," grabbed her coat, and tore across the beach. Joey and Rufus followed curiously.

"What's up?" asked Joe.

Jane did not answer. She was busy measuring off ten feet from the gnarly apple tree. It landed her knee deep in the water.

"Oh, the treasure!" Rufus remembered now.

"What treasure?" asked Joe.

"We had directions to dig ten feet from that crab-apple tree and we'd find buried treasure," said Jane mournfully.

"Who gave you directions?" asked Joe.

"Oh, some pirate," answered Jane absent-mindedly.

"And now the water's come where it's never been before,"
she said, shaking her head sadly and combing the bottom
of the ocean with her fingers and toes, trying to find her
little blue ring. All the children did dead man's float for a
long, long time, keeping their eyes open, hoping the water
would wash up the ring. But it never did. And gone now
was Jane's little blue ring and gone now was Rufus's box of
shells. Tears smarted Jane's eyes. She had loved that ring.
But of course she couldn't cry. After all, she could see that
what had seemed such an exciting idea before had turned
out all wrong.

"Well," said Rufus, "they're gone. And here comes the
Richard Peck!" he yelled.

It was time to go home. The three children wrapped the
coats around their shivering shoulders and, completely
water-soaked, they trod the hot pavement home.

Jane thought about her ring. Maybe a fish swallowed it.
She would make everybody go very easy when they ate their
fish, hoping it would turn up in one of them.

But she did forget about her ring for a time when she
reached home and found that Mr. Abbot had brought a
whole big wooden box full of fireworks. Night fireworks.

Skyrockets, Roman candles, and pinwheels! Great big ones! And finally the night-time did come, and one by one he and Joey set the things off into the air. Jane and Sylvie and Mama and Rufus sat on the porch and watched and burned sparklers, and they all exclaimed admiringly whenever a particularly pretty skyrocket spun up in the air with a hiss.

Mr. Buckle, the oldest inhabitant, shuffled up the path and sat down with them. He burned a sparkler too, and between the skyrockets and Roman candles, he led Rufus and Jane through the whole battle of Bull Run.

It was truly a glorious evening. And Rufus stomped up to bed tired and happy and wondering how he could wait until the next Fourth of July. But when Jane went to bed, she closed her eyes to go to sleep and she tried to remember what it was that made her heart heavy. Oh, her little blue ring. It would be nice to go to Mama and tell her about losing the ring, and hear her say, "There, there." But Mama was talking to the big people and Jane finally fell asleep, thinking, "Perhaps the little mermaid has found it. the little mermaid in Andersen's fairy tale."

10

THE FLYING HORSE NAMED JIMMY

"STAY ON, NOW," SAID RUFUS AS HE SETTLED THE CARD-board boy comfortably and safely on the back axle of his bike. His bike was really a tricycle, but of course he never called it that. "Stay on," he said, "and I'll take you for a ride." This cardboard boy was Rufus's friend and enemy. Friend when he needed a friend; enemy when he needed an enemy. Right now he was his friend and Rufus was taking him for a ride; a little ride down along the Green.

Rufus had picked the cardboard boy out of a pile of rub-bish outside the grocery store. Apparently the grocer did not want him any more. This cardboard boy was a familiar figure, for his picture was in every trolley car and news-paper. He was always offering a biscuit with a smile. The biscuits were cardboard too, not real, the same as the cardboard boy. He had on his same yellow rubber rain coat, rain hat, and boots that he always wore in rain or shine.

Today that was a good thing, for it was a very misty day in the late summer. Lots of worms had come out of the ground and lay around on the sidewalks. It must have rained during the night though it wasn't raining now and hadn't rained all day. It was just misty. Very, very misty and very quiet. Rufus rode down Raven Avenue and his ears rang from the quiet. He swallowed hard and his ears seemed to pop open. He pedaled slowly down along the Green, trying hard not to run over any worms.

"It's too bad I'm not goin' fishin'," thought Rufus. "Look at all the bait I'm wastin'." The worms were just ly-ing around tantalizing him. Rufus paused at the drinking trough for a drink and he surveyed the sidewalks. Half worms, quarter worms, and whole worms sprawled all over the place. Well, let them lie. He couldn't go fishing by himself. Mama didn't allow him to and the rest of the family was busy.

He got back on his bike. "Want to go home now? Or want to ride some more?" he asked his cardboard friend.

By rights Rufus should not go any farther than this on Raven Avenue, because this road led to Plum Beach where there was an amusement park. None of the Moffats was supposed to go down there alone. Sometimes they all went together on Saturday nights to see the fireworks and to ride the merry-go-round. Or on a sultry Sunday afternoon they might stroll down there to hear the band concert. But alone none of them ever went.

Rufus was not even thinking about going to Plum Beach now. But while he was sitting on his bike, swinging the pedal around, undecided as to what to do or where to go, he thought he heard the merry-go-round. Not very loud, just the faintest, softest sound of the music of the merry-go-round. "Sh-sh-sh, listen!" he said and he strained his ears. You couldn't often hear the merry-go-round this far away. Just once in a great while on a day such as today was, misty, soft, and quiet. But even today you couldn't hear it well. Now you heard it and now it seemed to disappear.

The music, faint though it was, made Rufus think about Plum Beach. He remembered that every time he had ever been there it was always bright and gay and jolly. It was jolly even on days when a sudden thunder storm scattered the crowds and made them dash, screaming and yelling, for the open trolleys, and it was exciting to watch the trolleys ride off, tipping precariously to one side as the throngs crowded the running boards and tried to get at least their heads inside.

Where Rufus was it was gloomy and quiet. But the faint strains of the merry-go-round seemed to say to him, "Here, it's fun." And then they faded out and Rufus pedaled slowly down another block, listening hard to catch them again.

"You hear the merry-go-round?" he asked his cardboard friend.

Rufus was fond of the merry-go-round. Who wasn't? But there was one horse in particular that he was very fond of. His name was Jimmy. He had his name, JIMMY, spelled out on his chest in red rubies. He was the only flying horse who had his name embroidered on him. A dappled-gray horse, he was.

"Want to see Jimmy?" Rufus asked the biscuit boy.

The cardboard boy had never been to Plum Beach. If

Rufus took the boy down there and showed him Jimmy and came right back, there would be no harm in that. "And do you think that Plum Beach is a hard place to get to?" he asked the cardboard boy. "You do? Wrong. It's easy. Straight down this same street all the way. No corners to turn. Nothin'. And just as easy to come back too. Nobody could get lost, not even a two-year-old." Besides, thought Rufus, we don't need to go into the park at all. We can just stand at the edge, at the gate, and look and listen. No, there was no harm in that at all. Just to the edge, that's what, and then home again.

"Come on," he said, putting a little steam into his pedaling. "Let's go. Hang on tight!"

Rufus rang his bell every few seconds. Since the top half of the bell was missing, it had a hollow rasping sound as though it had a cough. Rufus rode as fast as he could down Raven Avenue. Sometimes he stopped to listen for the merry-go-round which sounded less and less faint the nearer he got to it. No, it wasn't exactly like going alone to Plum Beach to go with this cardboard boy. He was really company.

"You want to see Jimmy, don't you?" he murmured.

Rufus rode past the car-barn where all the yellow trolleys were lined up and he didn't stop to look. The only trolley he stopped to look at was the Bridgeport Express which went sailing by. Now he could see the water of the Sound. Through the mist it was a dull gray.

Rufus had thought that the nearer he came to Plum Beach, the jollier the music would sound. The flying horses did sound louder, but they did not sound really jolly. In fact, they sounded disconsolate. Maybe he wasn't near enough to hear the fun and to smell the popcorn and peanuts. So he pedaled right up to the very gate of the amusement park. Yes, the water was gray and the day was gray and somebody had forgotten to turn off the electric lights over the gate that formed a circular sign, THE GREAT WHITE WAY, the name of the liveliest part of the park. But the pale electric lights looked no jollier than sparklers on the Fourth of July when you burn them in broad daylight instead of waiting for night-time.

Still it was probably lots of fun inside THE GREAT WHITE WAY. Inside he could watch the people shoot-the-chute into the water with a scream and a splash; watch the roller-boller-coaster swoop up and down and around, with people

238

screaming and yelling happily as they careened around the curves and took the big drop. But most of all he could watch his favorite flying horse named Jimmy.

Rufus had thought he would be able to see Jimmy from the gate. But he couldn't. The big thermometer that was called the high-striker stood in the way. You hit a disk at the bottom of this thermometer with a sledge hammer and tried to make it ring the bell at the top. If you rang the bell you got a big cigar. Once Joey had made it go half-way up, to a line marked "Try a little harder." But Rufus was not interested in this big thermometer. He was interested in Jimmy.

"I s'pose you're not satisfied," said Rufus to the cardboard boy. "Now you want to go inside, I s'pose. Watch the people have fun."

The cardboard boy, of course, never answered Rufus. He just looked eagerly ahead, always with the same pleasant smile and his hand outstretched, offering a biscuit. But Rufus did not need an answer. He wanted to see the people have fun himself.

So Rufus rode through the gate and into THE GREAT WHITE WAY. Here he expected gaiety, noise, music, laughing, and screaming. What he found was exactly the opposite. At first he did not realize this. The shoot-the-chute was going. The boats shot down into the water but nobody was in them. The roller-boller-coasters were tearing around. But nobody was in them either. The ferris wheel did have one single passenger. This was an old lady who had brought her knitting and was working away with an amiable smile as the ferris wheel wound aimlessly around and around.

"See that lady?" said Rufus to the cardboard boy. "She can knit and ride at the same time."

Rufus rode on. He could hear the water swooshing in the Old Mill, but no shrieks of delight came from inside. And there was the merry-go-round! The music was playing and the horses were prancing but there was not one single rider. Even so Rufus's heart beat faster when he saw Jimmy gallop into sight and then disappear around the other side. And he smiled and said, "See him?"

Rufus sat there watching the different amusements going. The roller-boller-coaster rattled over the tracks and looked almost like his and Joey's toy trains when they set them going and then sat back and watched. In fact, it seemed as though somebody had set all these things in

motion just to see them go.

Where was everybody who was supposed to be riding? That's what Rufus wanted to know. Whenever Rufus thought about Plum Beach, he thought of crowds of people. Now there was almost nobody around except the men who ran the place. They were keeping open from day to day, hoping to do a little more business before nailing everything up for the winter.

Rufus didn't know that things got nailed up at Plum Beach for the winter. He thought it was always noisy and jolly here. But gradually he began to realize that it was just as gloomy at the amusement park today as back in Cranbury, if not more so. In fact it was so gloomy that Rufus hoped he would not come across Jolly Olga. Usually he liked her. It was Joey who didn't. But even Rufus did not care to see her today.

Jolly Olga was a great big lady about as high as the second story of a house. She was a hollow lady, made out of painted plaster. She was a fake. A fellow stood inside of her on stilts and made her walk and shake hands. She had been made for a carnival once and the people who ran Plum Beach liked her so much, they said, "Let her stay. Let her wander around and shake hands with the children."

Jolly Olga! You'd be walking along with an ice-cream cone or a box of crackerjack and you'd be looking from side to side at the duck-shooting places, the penny arcades, or the Old Mill, then you'd turn around and there she'd be! Coming right toward you, nodding her great big head! Or you'd be watching the shoot-the-chute to see if you could spot Sylvie as she swooshed down into the pond, because the shoot-the-chute was Sylvie's favorite ride. And then you'd see Jolly Olga way across the pond and her shadow would ripple all the way back across the water at you.

Children were supposed to like Jolly Olga. Some did and some didn't. Joey was one of the ones who did not like her. He used to be scared of her. He used to try not to be scared because he knew she was a fake. But whenever she came around trying to shake hands with the Moffats, he kept his eyes on the bicycle acrobats on the tight-rope over the shoot-the-chute pond, or on the high-striker; and he pretended not to see her. He must have come upon her too suddenly once. She was so big that she could give a person quite a start if he wasn't expecting to see her. You could tell Joey she was nothing but a mask, an all-over mask, but it made no difference. Still he shuddered at just the name of Jolly Olga.

"Jolly!" he muttered. "What's jolly about her!"

As for Rufus, he neither liked nor disliked her. However, if he saw her today, he hoped she would stay over on the other side of the pond. He wasn't scared of her, but it was too gloomy a day to meet Jolly Olga. Certainly since he was the only person down here in THE GREAT WHITE WAY, if Jolly Olga saw him she'd probably want to shake hands. Who else could she shake hands with? Not the men who were running things. She was there just for the children. Besides, the men were busy outshouting one another with their cries.

"Step right up, ladies and gen'lemen. Guess your weight!" said one.

And the man at the high-striker cried, "Ring the bell and win a big cee-gar! Ring the bell and win a big cee-gar!"

"Step right up, folks, and win a ba-bee doll!" chirped the man in the duck-shooting pavilion. They were not real ducks. They were made of clay.

And the salt-water taffy man kept on making taffy, and the tall, thin man who was running the merry-go-round seized a dark red megaphone and bellowed through this every few seconds, "Step right up, folks. Five cents a ride!"

They all shouted and yelled and tried to drown out one another. Just practicing, thought Rufus, since there weren't any folks around. Just him. Do you suppose they were all shouting at him? He didn't have any money. Rufus turned his pockets inside out except for the one he kept his important things in, like his postcard from Al and the empty Bull Durham tobacco pouch. One look at his empty pockets and they could tell that he didn't have any money. Nevertheless, Rufus did feel a little embarrassed. People who came to THE GREAT WHITE WAY were supposed to ride things or at least buy a box of crackerjack. Well, he wouldn't stay long. He'd just get a little nearer to the flying horses, get a good look at Jimmy with the red rubies, and then he'd go home.

He rode closer to the merry-go-round. There was Jimmy! Rufus watched him gallop into view every time he came around those fake trees in the middle. What a horse! It seemed to Rufus Jimmy's big, soft, purple eyes saw him every time he came into sight; and as though Jimmy were laughing, he was so pleased to see him. He was the only horse Rufus ever rode. When Mama said he could have a ride on the merry-go-round, he always waited for Jimmy. If someone else got on Jimmy first, Rufus wouldn't ride that time. Not until he was free. Sometimes the Moffats had to wait for Rufus a long, long time until he was able to mount Jimmy. They didn't mind though. They liked to sit on the round bench at the edge of the merry-go-round and watch the horses and listen to the music.

"See him?" said Rufus excitedly to the cardboard boy every time Jimmy broke into sight.

"Step right up, folks!" yelled the man with the megaphone so loud Rufus couldn't help jumping.

". . . And win a ba-bee doll!" yelled somebody else.

". . . And win a beeg cee-gar!" from somebody else.

". . . Ladies and gen'lemen . . ."

They all yelled hard. Probably they figured that the louder they yelled the more likely they'd be to produce customers right out of space. Unless they were still yelling at Rufus. He pulled his pockets as inside out as he could make them, even the one with his important things. They might think he had money in that.

"There," he muttered. "I'm here just to look at Jimmy.

Nothing else."

Jimmy was so beautiful that, gloomy day or not, he looked as though he were sailing right over clouds. He really was sailing through clouds of mist. Rufus had been watching the flying horses so closely, dreaming about Jimmy, he hadn't noticed how thick the mist was getting. But all of a sudden he realized that he couldn't see the top of the high-striker any more. If Jolly Olga came along now, he imagined you couldn't see her head.

"Guess we better go," he said to the cardboard boy. But just as he was about to leave, somebody shouted, "Hey, kid, do you want a ride?"

It was the man with the megaphone. He was talking to Rufus.

"I haven't any money," Rufus replied.

"You can have a ride for nothing," said the man. "Maybe it'll bring some business, break our bad luck for the day."

"What about my bike?" asked Rufus.

"The ticket lady will watch it," said the man.

So Rufus wheeled his bike over to the ticket booth where the lady in a pink blouse said she'd mind it. Rufus picked up the cardboard boy and when the flying horses stopped he stepped on. He put the biscuit boy in one of the sit-down coaches drawn by two swans for, of course, the biscuit boy could not ride a horse. And he himself mounted Jimmy. The man strapped him on. Rufus did not like this as it interfered with his trying for the gold ring.

Rufus never had had so many rides on the flying horses before in all his life. One or, at the most, two rides were all he ever got. Now he rode and rode, around and around, and on and on. Jimmy . . . Rufus thought of Jimmy fondly and he patted his mane. He had red rubies on his harness too. Jimmy was the only horse in this merry-go-round that had his name right on him. He was truly a remarkable horse.

All of a sudden Rufus realized that he had had enough rides on the merry-go-round.

"Hey!" he yelled. "I want to get off." He was getting so dizzy he could no longer see the gold ring and the lady in the pink blouse was just a blur. But the music began again and the horses galloped on.

The next time the music reached the end of its tune, Rufus hollered again. "Hey, mister, I have to go home now."

But the long thin man with the megaphone paid no attention to Rufus. Either he did not hear Rufus or he pretended not to, in order to keep his one customer. Rufus looked back at the cardboard boy. He had slid into a half-reclining position in his chariot, but he was still cheerfully offering a cracker.

"Bet you're tired too," said Rufus.

Now the air looked very strange. Great clouds of vapor were puffing in from the water. Rufus yelled lustily and he tried to unfasten the heavy iron buckle of the strap himself. He began to bawl, in fact. Well, a boy who is bawling is not good for the trade either. That is what the long man must have thought, for he came winding in and out of the flying horses until he reached Rufus, and he unstrapped him. As the music came to a stop the man lowered Rufus to the floor. Rufus gave Jimmy a last pat. "Good-by," he said. Then he grabbed his cardboard boy out of the swans' chariot, and jumped off before the music could begin again and carry them around and around some more. He had had enough of·going around. His knees felt wobbly and his eyes crossed.

"Thanks for the rides," he said to the man with the

megaphone as he passed him on his way out of the pavilion. Rufus got his bicycle, and when his legs stopped shaking he pedaled slowly away with the cardboard boy once more perched safely on the back axle.

This was a real fog blowing in off the water, and Rufus realized it was high time he started for home. But there was just one more thing he wanted to see before he left Plum Beach.

"You want to see the boat that goes to Silver Sands?" he asked the cardboard boy. "And that's all," he warned him.

Right next to the merry-go-round was a long wooden pier from the end of which little white boats put off every half hour for an island called Silver Sands. If Rufus were lucky he might see one come in, see the captain put down the gang-plank with a thud; or watch one leave, churning up the water between it and the round posts that supported the pier. As he rode over the wooden planks they made a gulping sound. And between the wide boards, Rufus caught a glimpse of the dark green water lapping against the posts, all covered with barnacles and seaweed.

These glimpses of the world beneath the pier sent shivers up and down Rufus's spine. He pedaled very slowly and he stayed right in the very middle of the pier. Fog horns and boat whistles, some pitched high and some low, sounded their sudden warnings.

"Don't be scared," he said to the biscuit boy.

Rufus paused. He looked ahead. He did want to see the boat, but the fog was getting thicker and thicker. What was the use of going way out there to the end of the pier? You couldn't even see the lighthouse on the breakwater. You couldn't see anything. A nearby buoy tolled its melancholy bell and Rufus stopped short.

"All right, fellow," he said to his cardboard companion. "We'll go home now, if you'd rather. This is getting gloomy."

Rufus turned around in the tiniest possible area. He started pedaling back to land. Even on land the fog was very dense now. The flying horses were still going around but Rufus could hardly see them any more, and he could not distinguish Jimmy from any other horse. The ferris wheel had stopped and Rufus could only see the bottom seats. He hoped the lady who was knitting had not been left up in the air. None of the men was shouting any more. They had succumbed to the weather and had given up. It was quiet except for the forlorn music of the flying horses and for the steady blowing of the fog horns.

"It's just a fog," explained Rufus to his companion. "Everything is just the same, only you can't see it. That's all. Hang on. Don't be scared."

Rufus steered carefully straight ahead between the salt-water taffy stand and the Indian wampum stand and he rode on toward the gate that led out of THE GREAT WHITE WAY.

There was one thing that Rufus was really happy about. And that was that he had not seen Jolly Olga. He wasn't scared of Jolly Olga, but who would want to see her on a day like this? Not Rufus! All the same he said to the biscuit boy just to make conversation, "Sorry you didn't see Jolly Olga, the big lady," and presto! just as he said this, presto! there she was! Jolly Olga! Walking through the fog right towards him! Rufus stopped. He hoped she would not bump into him. He could just barely see her head, just the shadowy outline of it way up there in the fog.

Rufus crowded as close as possible to the soft shell crab counter. Goodness, how big Jolly Olga looked in this fog! She was so big she took up all the space. How was Rufus going to get past her and go home? She stopped in front of the soft shell crab stand, and she stayed there, hemming him in. At last Rufus rang his bell. Jolly Olga or no, he had to go home.

"Hey!" he yelled. He didn't know whether to yell, "Hey, mister!" or "Hey, lady!" He just said, "Hey!"

But the minute he yelled, Jolly Olga set her head to bobbing in her own inimitable manner and she bowed to Rufus and waved her hand. Jolly Olga never said anything. Just bobbed her head, shook hands, and appeared in unexpected places. That's all she ever did. That's what she did now, and then she disappeared in the fog. But Rufus saw the man inside. He was eating a soft shell crab sandwich.

"A fake," Rufus explained to his companion. "He eats. Who you like best, Jimmy or Jolly Olga?" he asked. "Jimmy," he answered his own question, as he steered his bike down the slope under the archway with the wan lights overhead that spelled THE GREAT WHITE WAY.

The last thing he heard as he left the desolate amusement park was the faint music of the merry-go-round. "Good-by, Jimmy," he said, and he headed for home.

"Don't be scared," he said to the cardboard boy. "It's

just one straight road home."

It's true it was spooky and gloomy riding in this fog. Usually Rufus knew right where he was. When he smelled coffee, he knew he was passing the A & P. He recognized the odor of the steam from the Chinese laundry and the leathery smell from the shoemaker's shop. But sometimes he really could not tell where he was and then he would take the postcard from the soldier named Al out of his pocket, hold it in his hand, and ride on, not quite so scared. Or at these times he would reach in his pocket for his empty Bull Durham tobacco pouch.

"Here, fellow," and his right hand gave the pouch to his left hand. "Put this in your pocket." And he remembered the day the ice-man gave it to him. "If you get scared, you can smell this tobacco," he said to his cardboard friend.

Gradually as he rode farther and farther away from Plum Beach, the music of the merry-go-round grew fainter and fainter. Then he didn't hear it at all.

Once the cardboard boy fell off. At first Rufus did not miss him, and when he did he wondered whether he should go back for him in all this fog. But of course he couldn't leave him behind, so back he turned. Fortunately he didn't have to go far before he found him. Rufus stopped and picked him up.

"Why don't you hang on?" he asked a little crossly. Then he settled the cardboard boy on the axle again, turned around, and steered for home.

On he went through the fog.

"Hope I don't miss Pleasant Street," said Rufus. And just then, *plinkety-plink, plinkety-plink!* Oh, the invisible piano player! Yes, there was only one music in the whole world that sounded like that to Rufus. He was glad to hear him play even though the invisible piano player was a fake too. Because that meant he was right back at Pleasant Street and home was just around the corner.

Rufus was cold and hungry and damp. "It's lucky you have your rain clothes on," he said to his companion. But if Rufus was glad to be nearing home, all the other Moffats would be gladder to have him there. They were standing on the little square porch, trying to pierce the fog with their eyes. Janey ran up and down the long green lawn.

"Rufus!" she called every now and then. He might be a couple of doors away and not know where he was. He might wander off, she thought, and never be seen again. She

thought of a sad, sad story she knew. This person was looking for that person. There was a fog or a blizzard. Nobody
could see anything and these two people came within a
dozen feet of each other and didn't know it and passed on
into the world, still searching . . .

"Rufus!" she called again and again, so he would not pass
right by his house and not know it. Then she listened.
What was that? Ding-ding! Ding-ding!

Rufus's bike bell!

"Rufus!" they all called. And as they yelled this time,
the mist lifted a little and Rufus burst through the fog like
a pony jumping through the paper hoop at the circus.

"Where have you been in all this fog?" Mama demanded.

"For a ride . . ." said Rufus.

11

POPCORN PARTNERSHIP

THE PEOPLE IN THE TOWN SAID IF THEY SAW, MUCH LESS
ate, another popcorn ball they would pop themselves. Nevertheless they considered it their patriotic duty to buy and
eat popcorn. Who started the popcorn craze in Cranbury?
The Moffats. Rufus and Jane Moffat, to be exact.

One day Rufus and Janey were sitting on the back fence
and they were thinking how they could become a Victory

Boy and a Victory Girl. To become one you had to earn money. Money given to you did not count. Not like war savings stamps where any money would do. To become a Victory Girl and a Victory Boy you must *earn* the money and give it to the War.

Rufus thought about this. If you had an aunt or an uncle who said, "Here, Rufus, here's fifty cents," you could not use that fifty cents to become a Victory Boy. But if the aunt or uncle said, "Here, Rufus, here's fifty cents for going to the store," that was all right to put toward your Victory Boy fund because you had earned it.

The most money Rufus had ever had he had found. That was the money in the ice. He didn't know whether he had earned it or found it. Both, he figured. He had found it and then he had worked to get it out. So if he found some more that way he could use it for the Victory Boy fund. However, there was no ice on the ground right now. It was the middle of October and in school Columbus had only just discovered America.

Jane racked her brain too. In the Alger books the heroes earned more money than anyone else she knew about. Phil the fiddler! She didn't have a fiddle. Tony the bootblack!

Everybody in Cranbury blacked his own boots, even the oldest inhabitant.

She thought about how other boys and girls were earning their victory buttons. Because once you were a Victory Girl you got a red button with V on it, and once you were a Victory Boy, a blue button. Some children were raking leaves, cleaning up back yards and cellars, and stacking the woodpiles. Jane and Rufus had already tried to do all of these things. But Cranbury was spotless. Everybody's cellar and back yard glistened, due to the furious onslaught of hundreds of these half-sized odd-jobs men.

Some children were going to get a fifty-cent piece for every "Excellent" they received on their report cards. In the Moffat family a hug or a kiss from Mama was what the children got for "Excellents." This was pleasant but did not help toward becoming a Victory Boy or Girl. Nancy Stokes was one of those who was getting fifty cents for each "Excellent." She offered to share her money with Jane because the two did their lessons together.

"If you didn't study with me, I probably wouldn't study at all," she argued. "And then I wouldn't get one single 'Excellent' and no money either."

Jane shook her head to this proposal.

"Well, the physiology 'Excellent,' if I get it, is really all yours because you explained the medulla oblongata to me."

But Jane was firm. Nevertheless, she asked Rufus about this. He thought she could take half of the physiology money but that's all. Jane still did not think so.

"No," she said. "But how *are* we going to earn the money?" Jane asked for the tenth time.

"The best way to earn money is to sell things," said Rufus. He was thinking of the men who came to the door selling things—the ice-man and the baker, the scissors sharpener and the vegetable man. He thought of all the money jingling in their pockets. All they had to do was reach in and pull out a handful.

"Yes," Jane agreed, "but what can we sell?"

"Peanuts," suggested Rufus, for he was very fond of these.

"No-o," said Jane thoughtfully, "because we don't have one of those things that whistle. But we could sell popcorn," she said.

So that's what they did. That was the way Jane and Rufus's popcorn business got started. And for some days it flourished. Jane did most of the popping. Some they rolled into popcorn balls and some they sold just hot and salted in paper bags. Mr. Buckle bought two bags the first week. He preferred the loose kind to the popcorn balls. For a while it looked as though popcorn was the very thing that all the residents of Cranbury had been waiting for, so fast did Rufus's and Janey's stock sell.

Then it was that the news of how Jane and Rufus Moffat were earning their Victory money spread and then it was that the whole town became flooded with popcorn balls. All the children dropped their rakes and brooms and stopped trying for "Excellents" on their report cards. All popped corn and trudged the streets; up this one and down the next, ringing door bells, and selling their popcorn balls. There was scarcely a house in Cranbury that did not have its bell rung at least a half dozen times a day by the popcorn vendors.

Janey and Rufus began to have considerable difficulty in selling their popcorn. The Moffats were having to eat more and more of it themselves at the end of the day.

"Don't pop so much," said Mama.

One Saturday they had walked miles to sell their pop-

corn, way up to Shingle Hill, in fact. They knew of a certain house up there and it was so far from town they felt no other children would have tried it yet.

"Of course no one would think to come way up here," said Jane as they puffed up the hill.

"Yes," agreed Rufus, "we might sell the whole basket."

But when they got there and rang the bell, the door opened and an unmistakable odor of popcorn greeted them. The people in this house were popping corn themselves. So Rufus and Jane hurried away and down the hill without having sold so much as one single popcorn ball on the whole long trip.

As they plodded wearily homeward, Jane said, "Now we ought to think of something else to sell. No one wants popcorn any more."

"Uh-hum," agreed Rufus.

But everything they thought of was popcorn or popcorn balls or had to do with popcorn. "I know what!" said Rufus, all of a sudden. His head had seemed empty. Then all of a sudden this idea had popped into it. He told the idea to Jane. They stopped to talk about it excitedly.

"What's the thing makes people like crackerjack?" he

demanded.

"The popcorn," said Jane, "and the peanuts," she added.

"Two things. But what's the real reason they like it?" he asked, and then answered his own question triumphantly. "Prizes!"

"O-o-oh!" Jane danced up and down as the possibilities of this idea raced through her mind. "We could make the prizes," she said.

"Sure," said Rufus.

The two children hurried home. Jane made some flour and water paste, got the scissors and paper and paints, and went to work. She was going to make pretty pictures, paste them on squares of bright-colored paper, and put one of these in each bag of popcorn. Rufus sat there wondering what he could make for prizes. He could make whistles. Whistles were very popular prizes in crackerjack boxes but they took too long to make. Once he had gotten a prize in a box of crackerjack and this prize was just a square piece of cardboard with the words "The world's your oyster," written on it.

"What does this mean?" he had asked Mama.

"It's your fortune," Mama had said.

Fortunes, that's what you called cards like that. "Shall I write fortunes?" he asked Jane.

She thought this was a wonderful idea. "Yes," she said, "everybody loves to have their fortune told."

So Rufus wrote fortunes. He wrote ten of them and on each one of them he wrote, "The world is your oyster."

Jane studied them. She thought they should not all be alike. "People don't all want the same fortune," she said.

So to each one Rufus added an extra fortune, such as "You'll be rich," "You'll be famous," "You'll be a fireman," "You'll be an ice-man," and several others. Jane agreed that these were fine.

Then they popped corn until they had filled every empty bowl and pot and pan. Naturally they needed plenty of popcorn. They were confident that the minute the news spread that a prize came with the popcorn these new packages would go like hot cakes.

"Put only one in each bag," she told Rufus. "It would be silly if someone got two fortunes, one saying 'You'll be a fireman' and another saying 'You'll be an ice-man.' How would they know what to believe?"

They then rolled a fortune into every popcorn ball. This

was even better than crackerjack, they thought.

At last they had finished. They piled the bags into a basket and out they went, thinking this time they would come home with their pockets full of money. Where would they go first? Why not begin here on their own street? They went up on Mrs. Price's porch and rang the bell. Unfortunately they were unable to get beyond the word popcorn. Mr. Price, who answered the bell, was kind, but no, he said, he and his wife had reached their full popcorn capacity. Jane and Rufus wanted to explain that this popcorn was different. It had fortunes and pictures—surprise popcorn. Mr. Price did not give them a chance. In fact nobody gave them a chance. The moment Jane said "Popcorn," the doors closed slowly but firmly.

Jane and Rufus passed other children with buttery-looking bags.

"They're not having any better luck," thought Jane. But goodness, what were they going to do with this superabundance they had popped for the day? "We'll sell them, but how?" Jane asked desperately.

By now they had reached the Green and their luck was not improving one bit. What should they do? Even the

Moffats would have a hard time eating up all this popcorn. Nevertheless, Jane and Rufus were about to go home for they heard the five o'clock whistle blow. Lights were beginning to come on in people's houses and in the store windows.

"If people only knew we had fortunes in our popcorn," mourned Jane.

First they stopped at the drinking trough opposite the Town Hall for a drink of water. In front of the Town Hall there was a big sign saying, "Re-elect Harvey Rollins for Town Selectman!" But Rufus and Jane paid no attention to that and were just about to leave for home when the big doors of the Town Hall swung open and lights streamed out into the street. Shouts, laughter, and talking burst upon their ears and then, presto, hundreds of men began to pour out of the Town Hall. It was a Town Meeting to hear all about Harvey Rollins.

"Oh, come on! Come on!" shouted Rufus to Jane. "All this many people haven't had any popcorn today."

He and Jane ran across the street. The men filed by, talking excitedly to one another. Some shouted angrily when they thought their companions disagreed.

"Look at the new sewers he built!" they exclaimed.

"And the new school!" added others.

But Rufus and Jane yelled above the men's voices.

"Buy some popcorn, mister! It's got prizes!"

First one man and then another did stop, and some bought popcorn balls and some bought loose popcorn. But in every case when they found their fortunes and read them aloud, they burst into loud guffaws. And many went home to dinner and their families in better humor than when they had left the Town Hall.

The pile of popcorn dwindled. Jane's voice became hoarse and Rufus's was getting shrill with excitement. The last man to leave the meeting was Mr. Buckle, the oldest inhabitant. Jane and Rufus had just one package left. "Let's give it to Mr. Buckle," said Jane.

And Mr. Buckle seemed delighted to have this popcorn, especially when he learned that there was a fortune or a picture inside. He opened his package with trembling fingers and felt around for his prize.

"You read this," he said to Jane when he found it.

" 'The world is your oyster. You will be a fireman.' "

"Fine! Fine!" said the oldest inhabitant. "Just what I've

274

always wanted to be." And he shuffled up the street eating his popcorn.

But Rufus and Jane sat down on the bench and counted their money. Now they had enough for their Victory buttons. And they went home tired and happy and hungry for their supper of baked beans—Rufus's beans.

12

A BONA FIDE VENTRILOQUIST

"WATCH ME!" SAID RUFUS, AS HE RAN PAST THE OLDEST inhabitant, and he stuck a knife right into himself up to the hilt. Of course the knife was a rubber one he had bought at Miss Twilliger's penny shop for two cents and it couldn't hurt a flea. But how could the oldest inhabitant know that? Or anybody else? It looked real.

"Did ya see that?" he'd ask, and plunge the rubber knife into his arm, stagger a bit, and laugh when people clutched their heads.

The truth of the matter was that Rufus was taking up magic. He hadn't been studying magic very long. But he knew three real tricks beside the rubber knife trick and he knew them well—the disappear-the-cards trick; the disappear-the-coins trick; and the handkerchief-and-match trick.

Jane knew one trick. It was a card trick the oldest inhabitant had taught her. Put two cards on the edge of the table, flip them into the air, have them turn a somersault, and catch them before they fell back down. That was her trick. It was not as good as the disappear-the-cards trick, but Rufus would have liked to master it. So far he hadn't been able to. He usually knocked the cards clear across the room in his desperate effort to catch them.

Not content with knowing the three magic tricks and the rubber knife stunt, Rufus was also working toward becoming a ventriloquist. Usually when he and Joey went over to the library, where it was nice and warm, to read, Joey would find the latest *Popular Mechanics* to see if silver foxes were still being advertised. And Rufus would find a book of magic and practice tricks and study ventriloquism.

What he hoped was that some day soon he would be able to throw his voice over to the other side of the room while all the time he was over on this side. Ventriloquism! That's what that was called. He practiced all the time.

Today Rufus was standing over by the apple tree, trying to throw his voice into the chicken coop. He hoped to be able to persuade Jane that there were chickens in the coop. Once or twice in the past the Moffats had had a few chickens, but right now, ever since last winter when their one little chicken, Melissa, had died of the pip, the coop was empty. There were still a few feathers around but there were certainly no chickens, and imagine what Jane would think when she heard "Peep! Peep!" coming right out of the chicken coop.

"Where'd the chickens come from?" she'd ask, and crawl through the long wire part of the coop to look at them. And then she'd back out wide-eyed, saying, "I was sure I heard a baby chicken." Then, "Peep, peep!" he'd say again, making his voice sound as though it were right at her very feet. And when she jumped, he'd yell, "They're invisible ones!"

"Peep, peep, peep," he practiced. He tried with his lips pressed together, with his tongue on this side, on that side, in the front, and in the back of his mouth. But it was no use. His voice stayed right with him and did not go where he meant it to.

Rufus climbed on top of the little chicken coop, pressing his fingernail in the tar paper, and prying off some of the flat round nail heads to use for fifty-cent pieces in his disappear-the-coins trick. He laughed as he planned all the wonderful times he could have when he really learned to be a bona fide ventriloquist.

For instance, they'd be sitting in school, quiet, his whole class, doing their arithmetic, say. Then suddenly, someone across the room—of course it would really be *him*, Rufus, the ventriloquist—well, that someone would say something like this, "Let me out! I want to go home!" The boy who sounded as though he were talking—let's see, it might be Harold Callahan—would jump a mile, and the teacher would say, "Harold, be quiet!" And then he, Rufus, would say again, "Hey, let me out!" And the place he had thrown his voice into this time was Harold's inkwell!

He'd have to be sure, planned Rufus, that the little sliding lid on Harold's inkwell was open, because he was not certain a ventriloquist could throw his voice into an inkwell if the top was closed. Oh, of course, he could. For instance, a ventriloquist could throw his voice into a closet even if the door was closed. That was one of the things that was most fun about ventriloquism, putting your voice into closed things and having people jump.

Naturally before the teacher decided to slap Harold's hands with a ruler, Rufus would make his voice come out of, let's see, come out of *her very own inkwell!*

Well! Rufus really roared at this thought, and while he was wiping the tears out of his eyes, Jane stepped through the gate in the fence, yelling, "So long," at Nancy Stokes.

"What are you laughing at?" she asked curiously, and laughing too because he was laughing so hard.

"Oh," sighed Rufus, "nothin'." He longed to try the "Peep! Peep!" in the chicken coop on Jane, but he knew he couldn't make his ventriloquism work yet. Instead he took his rubber knife out of his pocket. "Watch me!" he said and plunged it in his arm. Jane shrieked. She always did, even though she knew it was nothing but an old rubber knife anyway. And she ran into the house.

The next day during the arithmetic lesson, Rufus fell to thinking about ventriloquism. Most of the children were working hard, biting their pencils and ruling lines for the long division. Rufus had finished. The teacher was correcting spelling papers with her blue pencil. My, how fast she went! The room was very quiet. Rufus considered his plan of throwing his voice into somebody's inkwell. He looked across the room at Harold Callahan. Harold had finished with his paper, too, and was sitting with his hands folded, looking out the window.

In his mind, Rufus began to throw his voice across the room and into Harold's inkwell. It was getting easier. In his mind he did it better and better. Now he thought it had reached as far as Emma Ryder's inkwell, now across the aisle, now into Harold Callahan's inkwell. He practiced it and he practiced it inside his mind. Then he'd practiced it so long and so well inside his mind, he forgot he had not yet perfected ventriloquism in real life. He opened his mouth. "Let me out!" he said, thinking he was throwing his voice across the room into Harold Callahan's inkwell. He wasn't though. The voice that came out loud and startled the whole class was coming right from him, Rufus

Moffat. Everyone knew it. No one thought otherwise.

"Ruf-fus!" said the teacher in surprise. And the class, recovering from its startled amazement, burst into laughs. Rufus sucked in his lips and sat up straight and looked at his arithmetic paper, embarrassed.

Soon everybody was busy with arithmetic again. Or those who had finished sat with folded hands and waited. Emma Ryder was counting on her fingers and looking at the ceiling, desperately seeking the answer. Tick-tock, tick-tock, breathed the big round clock on the wall. Rufus forgot his embarrassment. He began to think again of the glorious days that would be his when he learned to ventriloquize. Now and then somebody scuffled his feet or dropped a book. But Rufus did not hear. He was completely lost again in a world where he was the great Houdini, and he was throwing his voice here and he was throwing his voice there; throwing his voice from Rufus in the fourth seat in the fourth row, now to the closet in the front of the room where boxes of chalk and piles of erasers were kept, and now to the inkwell on the teacher's desk.

"Let me out!" he said, practicing out loud the words he had been practicing in his mind, and forgetting again this was school and no talking out loud without first raising your hand.

Well! This time the teacher really was annoyed. "Rufus Moffat!" she said sternly, and at her tone of voice the class quickly swallowed its laughs and sat up straight.

"The teacher thought I did it again to make 'em laugh," thought Rufus ruefully, as he stood in the corner of the cloakroom where he'd learn how to behave himself.

Up and down the long corridor there were one or two other boys standing in the cloakrooms that belonged to their classes. They stood there desolately and wondered when it would be time to go home. Rufus wondered why they were standing there. Had they tried to be ventriloquists too?

You might think that this experience would have dampened Rufus's interest in ventriloquism. Not at all. He practiced harder than ever, though he was careful to do all his practicing outdoors and not during the arithmetic lesson.

Fortunately about this time Miss Twilliger's penny shop laid in a supply of ventriloquists' disks. These disks were made of rubber and tin. "Learn how to use your SECRET POWER," read the words on the cardboard they were attached to. You put one of these disks on your tongue and you soon learned to ventriloquize. Vox Pops, they were called. They cost one cent. Rufus did not buy one the minute Miss Twilliger put them in the store. He studied them through the store window for a long time. At first he thought it was cheating to ventriloquize with a Vox Pop in his mouth instead of only his tongue. Then he thought, "I'm crazy. How do swimmers learn to swim? With water wings, of course. Lots of them do, anyway. They begin on water wings and soon they are able to swim without them after they get their arms and legs going the right way."

Now take a Vox Pop. Rufus would ventriloquize with this disk in his mouth for a while. Then he'd get rid of the thing and he'd be able to go right on ventriloquizing without it. It was not cheating. Like water wings, a Vox Pop was a way of learning. He went in and bought one.

He waited until he got home in his back yard to try the Vox Pop. He climbed onto the chicken coop and carefully placed the disk on his tongue. "Peep! Peep!" he tried first. He made his voice high and low, loud and soft, attempting to throw his voice all over the yard and under the house. But all the voices came from right there on the chicken coop and nowhere else.

Rufus was not discouraged. It is true that with water wings one can learn to swim almost immediately. At least float. But with these disks one could not ventriloquize right away. However, the art of ventriloquizing is much more difficult to learn and consequently much less common than the art of swimming. Otherwise the world would be full of ventriloquists. Rufus reasoned this way as he made his voice sound like a bullfrog and tried to place it in the puddle by the rain spout.

He laughed out loud, his spirits soaring as he thought that when he got really good he could say ba-room, ba-room! like a frog. Then he'd put the ba-room in Harold Callahan's inkwell or the teacher's.

Rufus climbed down and went over to the doorway of the barn. The Moffats' museum was what the family called the barn now because it had so many of their old possessions in it. Sylvie's old brown bike they'd all learned to ride on was in one corner. It didn't have any tires any more and the wheels and spokes were bent. The seat had fallen off and the bell didn't ring. Mama was going to sell it to the junk man.

"Oh, no," cried Jane. "We'll put it in the barn and call the barn a museum. We'll have the Moffats' first bike on view, the way they have the first fire engine in the Cranbury Historical Society."

So that's the way the museum started and the Moffats kept their mounted bugs there and Rufus kept his cardboard boy at the doorway. He was the guard. He was supposed to keep you from touching things.

"Have a biscuit," said Rufus now, wishing he could throw his voice into the biscuit boy's smiling face and surprise everybody. "What!" everybody would say. "A cardboard boy can talk!"

Rufus was bound to admit, as the afternoon wore on and twilight came, that he had not improved one iota in ventriloquism even with a Vox Pop in his mouth.

But he wasn't giving up being a real ventriloquist.

Not yet.

He clicked his ventriloquist's disk around in his mouth, trying it in this position and that. It had taken some time for him to learn to ride Sylvie's old bike, and then all of a sudden he had just ridden off. Vox Pop would be like that. Probably all of a sudden he'd hit it right. Goodness, no; he had not given up being a ventriloquist yet.

That very evening, in fact, something happened to encourage Rufus. He had gone into the little green and white parlor to practice his ventriloquism all by himself. The rest of the family were tired of hearing him. He sat in the big armchair with his legs over the arm and he said, "Get out of there, you!"

He no longer aimed his voice at any special spot. He would be content for his voice to land anywhere now just so long as it didn't seem to come right from him.

He practiced and practiced and all the while he was practicing Jane and Nancy Stokes were sitting on the little square front porch, talking. They were talking in such low voices that Rufus did not even know they were out there.

"Rufus is so funny," laughed Jane. "He spends all his time talking to himself. He wants to be a ventriloquist."

"What does he say?" Nancy laughed too.

"Oh," said Jane, "he usually says the same thing, 'Let me out' or 'Get out of there, you!'"

Now when Jane said "Let me out" and "Get out of there, you!" she unconsciously raised her voice to sound like Rufus.

And it did sound like Rufus. In fact, it sounded so much like Rufus that it roused him from his armchair like a bolt of thunder. "Criminenty!" he exclaimed. "That's it!"

His voice! Way out on the porch. "Let me out!" as plain as day. He was getting so he could make it work! This Vox

Pop wasn't so bad after all. The funny part was he hadn't even known he'd said it that time. He hadn't even opened his mouth. He'd been thinking it plenty, of course. Maybe he had said it. He must have said it! He could ventriloquize

now! He took the little disk out of his mouth, wiped it off fondly, and stuck it in his pocket. Tired and happy and almost ecstatic, he climbed the stairs to bed.

In school the next day the whole class was having a silent reading period. When the children finished reading to the bottom of the page, they would have oral reading. The teacher hoped that then, out loud, they would whiz along fast. Rufus finished his silent reading. In fact he finished the whole story because it was a good one about the Minotaur. Then he sat there with his hands folded, the way he should. And then he remembered about last night. He smiled to himself. He was getting good now. Not perfect yet, because in some ways his voice had sounded like an echo. Still it was a good beginning.

Of course, Rufus was not going to try ventriloquism in the schoolroom again; not after that unfortunate experience the other day when he had to stand in the cloakroom. But he could not resist putting his Vox Pop in his mouth and trying it in this position and that and remembering where it was on his tongue last night when his voice jumped out on the porch. He had to be careful, naturally, for the teacher might think he was putting some candy in his mouth. As a matter of fact, Hughie Pudge did think Rufus was eating a Boston wafer and held out his hand under the desk, wanting a piece.

Rufus pressed his lips together, shook his head, frowned and held out his hands with a gesture that was meant to say, "I haven't any," and then he slipped back into his dreams of ventriloquism, while Hughie continued to eye him with suspicion and reproach.

Rufus turned the disk over in his mouth. This was the way he had had it arranged last night, he thought. Gosh! He wished it would work that way all the time. Maybe it would. How did he know? He should have kept on doing it last night once he had the hang of the thing. He wished he could try it now. Why shouldn't he try it? What was he, scared? Scared of standing in the cloakroom? But he wouldn't have to stand in the cloakroom again. He was a real bona fide ventriloquist now.

"Let me out!" he said boldly, in a high squeaky voice. He tried to sound like some funny little thing that got caught in the inkwell on the teacher's desk.

While the storm was gathering on Miss Lumkin's face and Rufus was scrunching himself into a small ball, feeling more than uncomfortable, in walked Mr. Pennypepper, the Superintendent of Schools; not just of this school, of all the schools in the town of Cranbury.

"What do you think," said Miss Lumkin to the Superintendent, "of a boy who says 'Let me out' all the time when it is good and quiet in the classroom?"

Apparently Mr. Pennypepper didn't know what to think! He just stood there, rocking back and forth on his toes, clinking the coins in his pocket and looking at the ceiling. Then he shook his head and said, "Will that boy rise, please?"

Rufus arose.

"Explain yourself," said Mr. Pennypepper

Rufus could not talk because he had his Vox Pop in his mouth. He did not think to take it out. To all questions he was silent, and finally Miss Lumkin suggested there was a possibility that Rufus not only had been talking out loud, saying "Let me out!" whenever he saw fit, but also that he had his mouth full of candy.

"Put it in the wastebasket," the teacher said.

Rufus walked to the front of the room, the whole class holding its breath and everybody glad he was not in Rufus's shoes.

Mr. Pennypepper stood by with folded arms and watched Rufus open his mouth and drop what he had in it into the basket.

"I would suggest," said Mr. Pennypepper, looking back at the ceiling, "that this young man be sent to my office."

The entire class sucked in its breath, like one person. Standing very straight Rufus went out of the room and down the hall to the little round office where Mr. Pennypepper did his work and interviewed the bad. This office was in the rounded corner of the building, the part that was built like a castle. Rufus had been here only once before in his whole life when he brought a certificate from the Board of Health saying he was all over scarlet fever and could go back to school. Rufus looked around and he wondered where Mr. Pennypepper hung his strap. He was glad he didn't see it anywhere. All the same, to keep his courage up he clutched his ragged old postcard from the soldier named Al.

Mr. Pennypepper soon came in. He did not sit down. He rocked from heel to toe and he looked at the ceiling. Finally he took something out of his pocket.

"What is this thing called Vox Pop?" he asked.

"It's a thing you put in your mouth," murmured Rufus.

"What is it for?" he asked.

"For ventriloquisms," said Rufus.

"I see," said Mr. Pennypepper.

"Now it's coming," thought Rufus. In the cases of very bad children Mr. Pennypepper did sometimes have to strap them.

Mr. Pennypepper studied Rufus and he studied Vox Pop which he held in his hand on a piece of paper. Finally he said, "There is a time and a place for everything, young man. Put this in your pocket and leave it there. Understand?"

"Yes, sir," said Rufus.

"Now," said Mr. Pennypepper, rubbing his hands and looking stern, "go back to your room!" He said all this as though he had just been through a terrific ordeal.

Rufus went back to his room and the class could not take their eyes off him for the rest of the day. Had he been strapped or hadn't he been strapped? That's what they all wondered.

Rufus felt chastened. He had a good mind to throw Vox Pop into the wastebasket once and for all and never use it again. No matter how you looked at the thing, it was a fake. Still he didn't like to throw it away, and he could keep it in the Moffats' museum next to the mounted bugs. So he put it back into his pocket.

But he never did try to make voices come out of inkwells again; not in school at any rate. In fact, he gave up trying to be a ventriloquist—at least for a day or two. Then he took it up again and he continued with the study of magic.

"Watch me!" he'd say to anyone who would look, and he'd plunge the rubber knife into the palm of his hand.

13

BETTER TIMES ARE COMING NOW

"YES," SAID MAMA TO THE CHILDREN, "BETTER TIMES ARE coming now for all people."

Why? Because the war was over. Peace had come. This was the way it happened. A few days ago, in the middle of Rufus's reading lesson, all of a sudden the whistles blew! Whistles and sirens and fire alarms! Church bells of all the four churches rang, peal after peal! All the children looked at the teacher. What was the matter?

The teacher's face broke into a half-believing look of joy. "The war is over," she exclaimed. And her eyes filled up with tears as she looked at the flag behind her over the blackboard, a flag with four blue stars in it, one for each of her four soldier brothers.

Then the class went wild with joy and just as the big boys in the back of the room were about to throw erasers back and forth, in walked Mr. Pennypepper himself, smiling and clinking the keys in his pocket. Rocking from heel to toe and looking at the ceiling the way he always did when he gave a speech, he said, "The war is over! We have won the war! Everybody go home."

So everybody went home. And all the bells rang for a long, long time. But then it seemed that something was wrong. And a little later it was found that the war was not over. A mistake had been made. The armistice had not been signed. The bells should stop ringing. Peace had not come. Everybody must live as they had been living before they thought there was peace.

"Should we go back to school?" asked Rufus, thinking this must be like a fire drill.

But no. Since the children were all home now, they might just as well stay home, the teachers and the mothers decided. And they all tried to forget how happy they had felt for those few hours while they had been thinking there was peace.

The next day everybody went back to school and there was reading and writing as usual, and the people bought victory stamps, and in the Moffats' house they were still dividing the butter evenly to make it go round, and the men returned to work and did all their usual jobs. And then a few days later Rufus was standing in the front of the room about to sing his slip. He had just discovered to his relief that it was not in six-eight time. He raised his arm to beat time and he opened his mouth to sing. Then all of a sudden there they were again! All the whistles, church bells, sirens, school gongs, going like sixty. The war was over again.

"The war is over," the teacher said hopefully, "and this time it must be true."

Again the whole school was let out. At first everybody was very careful not to become too excited in case this might be another false alarm. But soon it became evident it really was so. The war *was* over. A real armistice had been signed, and this was November the eleventh and would become a famous day.

"I guess they had that first armistice day," said Rufus to Hughie Pudge, "to see if people would like peace or not. Like a rehearsal. If they liked it, they'd do it for real."

When Rufus reached home he stomped up on the porch noisily, stepped over Mr. Abbot's rubbers, flung the door open and clattered through the house to the kitchen, avoiding the dining room where the sewing was going on.

Jane was in the kitchen, squeezing the orange coloring out of the tiny little gelatin football that was supposed to make the oleomargarine look just like butter. Then she took a fork and tried to mash the coloring into the margarine evenly. Soon the white margarine became streaked with orange, but it didn't look like smooth butter yet.

"It's because it's so hard," Jane murmured to herself. Jane didn't pay any attention to Rufus who always entered the house in this noisy fashion, giving one the impression that all doors and windows had suddenly been flung wide open and great gusts of air let loose in the house. Jane was thinking about what Mama had said when she came home from school.

"Better times are coming now for all people," Mama had said. It sounded good to hear Mama say that.

Jane didn't pay any attention to Rufus and Rufus didn't pay any attention to Jane. He seemed to have something on his mind. He really did have something on his mind. He was pleased the war was over. Not only because they had had two afternoons off from school—the mistake last Thursday and the real thing today—but also he had a certain plan in his head. A couple of years ago Rufus had gotten a letter from Santa Claus telling him, "Sorry, all the ponies are at the war." Well, the war was over now, wasn't it? That meant they didn't need all the ponies any more.

Rufus was thinking of a soldier friend, the fellow he gave his washcloth to at the station. He took the card this soldier had sent him out of his pocket and examined it for the millionth time. It had come all the way from France, and all it had on it was Rufus M., Room Three, School, Cranbury, Conn., U.S.A.! Naturally the fellow didn't know Rufus's last name because all Rufus had printed on the paper was Rufus M. But he got the card all the same. It was old and bent but you could still read it.

Now all Rufus knew about this soldier was his name, Al. Al what? Just Al. Rufus didn't even know as much about Al as Al knew about him. He tossed his red mackinaw on a chair and sat down in the wicker rocker in front of the stove. Catherine-the-cat was sitting on the little door over the grate, and she blinked rather amiably, for her, at Rufus.

Rufus rocked hard.

It would be a good idea to write that soldier in France,

that's what Rufus was thinking; see if he could bring a pony back with him, now that the war was over. If it wasn't any trouble, that is. But Rufus knew better than to send a letter to just "Al in France." Still the important thing was to get the letter written; then he might think of some way of getting it to him.

Rufus felt around in his pocket. He found an old stub of a pencil and one of his arithmetic papers. On the back of it he wrote,

"Dear sojer. If they don't need the ponies any more over there, could you bring one back with you? Thanks for the postcard. It got to me."

Then he printed Rufus M. He could have written the *offat* part of Moffat as easy as pie but the soldier knew him only as Rufus M. That's the way the soldier wrote to him. So that's the way Rufus signed it. He looked at his letter and he thought how could he send it? He rocked and thought, but in the end he was bound to admit he knew of no way to get this letter to Al.

So he lifted the lid of the stove and dropped the letter in. The fire had burned low and there were dull red coals only in the middle. With a puff Rufus's letter caught on fire and burned up. Even after it burned you could still see the lead writing on the charred paper. Then a sudden draft whisked the letter over to the side where the dead ashes were. Rufus left it there, knowing eventually it would float up the chimney. And who knows? Maybe the soldier in France would somehow get the message, or maybe Rufus would learn some way of addressing a real letter to him. He clapped the lid back on with a clank and went over to the kitchen table to watch Jane struggle with the oleomargarine.

After Jane had mixed the margarine properly, Mama would divide it evenly into seven parts, one for each day of the week, because it had to last a week. Then she would divide each of the seven parts into five portions, one for each of the Moffats, and that small piece was supposed to be his share of butter for the day. It was always hard to decide whether to eat one slice of bread with plenty of butter on it and enjoy it or spread it very thin and make it last all day. Sometimes the children decided one way and sometimes the other.

Sylvie rushed in from the little green and white parlor Her cheeks were bright and her eyes were sparkling.

"Thought you were in the sitting room," said Jane.

"No," said Sylvie.

"Where's Mr. Abbot?" asked Jane.

"Oh," said Sylvie carelessly, "I don't know. Talking to Mama in the sitting room, I suppose."

She danced over to the stove and sat down in the wicker rocker. She looked at a piece of paper she held in her hand and she smiled to herself. Then she jumped up. She crumpled the paper, lifted the lid of the stove, and dropped it in. It lay there a moment without burning and grew brown around the edges. Then it burst into a bright flame. Sylvie's eyes shone as she watched it. The lead writing was still visible even after her paper had all burned up into a delicate black wisp. And what she'd written on her paper was Sylvie Abbot. That's all. Sylvie Abbot all the way down the page as though she were learning to write a new name. Her lips formed the words as she read them on the charred paper. Sylvie Abbot. It was pretty. She watched the words for a long time with a faint smile. Then she slowly placed the lid back on the stove and she danced over to the kitchen table.

"I'll help you," she said to Janey. She took the fork out of Jane's hand and gave the margarine a few pats herself. But she was too excited to work long She jabbed the fork into the bowl and danced off around the room singing, "Tit Willow, Tit Willow."

"Thank goodness, she doesn't sing screetchy like most ladies," thought Rufus.

Jane picked up the fork again and she watched Sylvie curiously. She jabbed the fork viciously into the margarine. She felt uneasy. She had a feeling there was going to be a change in the Moffats' house. She felt this was going to be a bigger change than any they had had since they had moved away from the yellow house on New Dollar Street to this house. She became lost in her thoughts and scarcely heard Joey come in the back entry.

Joey was the last one home. He had been out, all over town, selling Extras and delivering papers to his regular customers. He slung his canvas paper-bag on top of Rufus's coat and sank into the wicker rocker. Creak. Creak. It crackled and creaked as he rocked. He felt tired. It was good to be sitting down in front of the fire. He watched a tiny red coal drop now and then into the grate. He looked at the coals and he fell to dreaming. The war was over. PEACE in big letters all over the front of the paper. Just PEACE. No other words at all. Better times were coming for all people. He remembered what Mama had said. The words sent a warm glow through him.

Soon he could start raising his silver foxes and he planned to buy a motor boat some day. Put-put-put-put-put. They'd put-put all over the Sound. He'd only just gotten this idea about a motor boat; saw a picture of a beauty in *Popular Mechanics* the other day—one big enough for all the Moffats. A cabin in it, even. Could sleep in it and eat. There was a little stove with two burners. He'd keep the engine shining. Whew! He was tired. He rested his head back on the wicker chair, his eyes half closed. Through his lashes he watched the bright coals but he wasn't really seeing them. He was seeing the silver foxes he'd have, and the motor boat going all over the harbor and out in the Sound too. They'd go farther than Stony Creek—go up the Quinnipiac or the Housatonic. He'd always wanted to go up rivers. . . .

Joey took a smudgy piece of paper and a pencil out of his pocket. He figured and figured about his boat and his foxes. Then when he heard someone coming, he quickly crumpled up his paper, for the foxes and the boat were his own secret plans, lifted the lid of the stove, and dropped it in. The paper began to smoke and then puff! it caught on fire. Joey watched it burn, while the flame threw lights and shadows all over his face. The fire was so bright the red coals seemed dusty and old in contrast. Even after Joey's paper had burned he could see the figures he'd been making about foxes, and he could see the pencil sketch of the motor boat he'd made. Joey smiled out of the corner of his mouth. Good things—motor boats and silver foxes. He replaced the stove lid almost lovingly and stepped to the kitchen table, made Janey move over, spread out one of his papers, and started to read.

Jane's arm ached and her hands ached. This margarine was so hard! She just couldn't get the orange coloring to mix in properly so it looked like real butter. It looked streaky and mottled. Some places there was a lot of color. Some places there was none. She took the bowl and placed it on the stove. Perhaps if the margarine melted a little it would be easier to mix. She sat down in the wicker rocker and waited for it to soften.

She put her hand in the little groove in the right hand side of the little rocker. This was Mama's sewing chair and there were spools of thread, a thimble, scissors, a tape measure, and even a pencil here. Jane's fingers absent-mindedly closed on the pencil. It was a good one with a sharp point. It must be one of Joey's, for his pencils always had good points on them. She moved around in her chair, getting really comfortable and putting her feet on the edge of the stove. She was sitting on a piece of paper and it crackled along with the chair every time she moved. She drew it out from under her and looked at it aimlessly. It was a part of one of Rufus's arithmetic papers. Jane drew some pictures on the paper and then she began writing some words. The words she wrote, the first ones that came into her head, were the words Mama said when they came home from school that day, "Better times are coming now for all people."

Those were good words to write, thought Jane. And when they came true maybe she wouldn't have to mix that little football of coloring into the oleomargarine any more. Maybe they'd have real butter and they wouldn't have to divide each pound into all that many pieces either. They wouldn't have to think whether to spread it thick once and eat it pleasurably or spread it thin so it'd last all day. And sugar! There'd be real sugar, not this brown stuff. And good real hard black coal. No more of this by-two-minutes kind. Better times . . .

Well, her margarine looked as though it were softer now. Jane stood up. She lifted the lid of the stove and she dropped her paper in it.

"Look at the way it's burning," she told herself. "You can see the words still, even though the paper's all burned up."

Then she noticed the other burnt papers, so thin they looked like black tissue paper now. On one she could see a picture of a boat. She looked at it curiously. Joey was always drawing pictures of boats. And this other piece of paper had Rufus's name on it. Rufus M. His paper had curled all up. Janey took the poker and gently turned it over to see what was on the other side. But as she did so it fell to pieces and she would never know what else he had written.

Anyway she lost interest in Rufus's paper for her eye had caught sight of still another bit of writing. In a corner of the stove she saw Sylvie's round handwriting. Just her name. *Her* name? Not *her* name—Sylvie Abbot over and over. Sylvie was Sylvie Moffat, not Sylvie Abbot. Oh! She

was trying it out to see how it sounded. That proved it. What she'd been worrying about was true. If Sylvie liked the sound of the name, Sylvie Abbot, she was going to keep it. Jane scowled back the tears. She didn't want Sylvie to get married; not to anybody; not to Mr. Abbot who left his overshoes on the porch every day; and not to the red-headed sailor at sea either, who still sent Sylvie letters even though Mr. Abbot tap-tapped with his toe every time one came.

It would be dreadful if Sylvie got married and moved away and went somewhere else. For one thing, who would take care of Janey's chilblains? She remembered how many times Sylvie had come up to bed while she was still awake because her toes itched so. And Sylvie would take first one foot and then the other in her cool hand and hold it. Then for a while they would feel better. But now Jane did not have time to stay sad for long. She heard the front door open and close. Mr. Abbot! Going now. And Mama came briskly into the kitchen.

"Well!" she exclaimed. "Is this where everybody is? But isn't it getting cold in here?"

She took the poker from Janey and dug at the fire from

below. "What's the matter with everybody?" she asked. "Four able-bodied children practically sitting right on the fire and it's going out. Jut because Sylvie is planning to marry Jack Abbot and, mind you, even that's not going to happen for a year or so at least, that's no reason," said Mama, "to let the fire go out."

Silence greeted Mama's statement while all the children were taking it in and sorting it out in their minds but outwardly going on with what they were doing before Mama spoke, as though she had said nothing. Jane felt relieved. After all, a year or so is a long time. Life could go on just the same for a long, long while until everybody got so used to the idea of Sylvie Abbot that it wouldn't seem bad any more.

Mama took all the lids off the stove. She picked up a piece of Joey's newspaper that had fallen to the floor. She crumpled it up a little and laid it on the cooling coals to start the fire up again. The paper rested on the dull ashes a moment and then it burst into a blazing flame. As it began to die down, Joey came over to the stove with an armful of shavings. Rufus followed him because he liked to watch the fire start up again.

"Look!" he exclaimed in excitement. And all the Moffats drew around the stove and looked in. They looked at the word that stood out of the burnt sheet of newspaper. In

tremulous, rippling letters lit by a last glow from the burning paper, as though it were seen through the water of the ocean, was the one word PEACE, the headline of Joey's newspaper.

Mama looked at the word and all the children looked too, silently. Then Mama said again, "Yes, you know what that means, don't you? It means better times are coming now, for all people."

And she took the poker and gently scattered the charred fragments of the newspaper and of the papers on which the children had written, so that all the dreams and wishes and plans of the Moffats were gathered in a little pile in the middle of the stove where they soon were wafted up the chimney and became part of the air.